From the Cross Paranormal Files

Kindred Spirits

Wanda Hargrove

2017 ©   Wanda Hargrove

No part of this may be reproduced without the author's consent.
This is a work of fiction. Names, places, characters, and incidents are the product of the author's imagination or used fictiously. Any resemblance to persons living or dead is entirely coincidental. Any resemblance to business establishments, locales is coincidental.

Other books written by Wanda Hargrove.
The Larkwood Series:
Blood Relations
Trials and Tribulations
The Dutton Trial
Not yet released but coming soon
The Wolf in the Hen House

From the Cross Paranormal Files:
Kindred Spirits

Dedications

This book is dedicated to my friends and family. Also, to my mentor Roberta Simpson Brown. I couldn't have done this without you cracking that whip last year and telling me to write.

I need to give a huge bow to a very good friend of mine, who let me toss ideas at her and she gave me her feedback, Erika Outcast.

Kindred Spirits

Wanda Hargrove

Chapter 1

Jasmine Stone brushed a strand of her strawberry blond hair out of her eyes. Her caramel skin gave a hint to her Cherokee heritage, but the reddish blonde hair also hinted at Scottish and Irish heritage. She had things to do today, and one of those things was to walk her dog, Bella. She grabbed the leash from the nearby table, "Come on Bella."

Bella ran in from the other room. She was called tri-colored, but she was mostly black but with some reddish tan on her eyebrows, jaws, legs, and stomach. White ran down her muzzle and a white spot on her chest and across the top of her paws and running some up her legs. The white on her chest resembled a ghost shape. Bella was a Greater Swiss Mountain Dog, and she was good at alerting Jasmine to the presence of dark or demonic spirits if she didn't notice them first.

She knew her mother and father weren't thrilled with the work she did with the paranormal, but it gave Jasmine a sense of accomplishment especially at being able to help people who needed it. She hooked the leash to the dog's collar and pulled the door open to her apartment. She opened the door and stared at her younger sister, Katie.

Katie could be called the black sheep of the family and took after the Native American side more than Jasmine. Katie had the black hair and darker skin. Both sisters had the brown eyes, but Jasmine's were a shade lighter with a few flecks of what looked like shining gold when a person looked at her the right way.

Jasmine took a step back and frowned. Her sister had her hand raised to rap on the door, but of course, she wasn't paying attention. "What are you doing here?"

Katie shoved her sunglasses on top of her head, "I need a place to stay for a day or two."

Jasmine shifted her weight from foot to foot, "Bella needs a walk. Join us, and you can explain why you're on my doorstep." She pushed past Katie, shut her door, and locked it. She stuffed the key into the pocket of her jeans and led Bella down the steps with Katie walking behind them.

Jasmine led Bella into a grassy area between apartment buildings populated with a few small trees. A light breeze sifted through the leaves, and the grass and shade brought some relief to the July heat. "Now, you can explain why you're here."

Bella sniffed around the area and circled around several times until she found the perfect spot to do her business.

Katie stared into Jasmine's brown eyes, "I needed to get away. Mom's on my case again, and dad is just ignoring everything I say."

Jasmine waved her hand as if to say speed it up.

Katie sighed and rolled her eyes, "I'm in love, and they won't listen to me at all."

Jasmine put her hands on her hips, "Who is it?"

"Max."

Jasmine's eyes bulged, and she gasped, "You can't be serious."

Katie grabbed her older sister by the shoulders, "Of course I'm serious." A dreamy smile sat on Katie's face, "He's seriously hot."

"Have you gone insane. He's ten years older than you!" Jasmine shook her head and rubbed her temple. Her sister was seriously giving her a headache. She glanced down at her watch. She needed to get back to work, being an entrepreneur making Native American Jewelry and other items did pay the bills and allowed her to live comfortably, but it didn't her much time for a social life. "I'm busy, but you can't stay with me this time. Go to one of your friends and stay there for a while."

Katie's voice wavered, "I knew it! I should never have come here," she stuck her finger in her sister's face, "You better not tell mom and dad I was here. I know they're looking for me," she spun on her heel and stomped away. She shook her hands up in the air as if she were having a silent conversation with someone.

Jasmine tugged on Bella's leash, "Come on, let's get out of this heat."

Spencer Cross sat behind his giant Mahogany wood desk. He glanced at the screen of his laptop. He couldn't find anything interesting on YouTube. His eyes roved around the matching mahogany paneled walls, the window that looked out onto the street where the road shimmered from the blistering heat outside as the sun beat down mercilessly. The area was grasped in the usual mid-July heat wave of temps around one hundred.

He was grateful that the AC worked just fine at keeping his house to a controlled seventy-four degrees. He spun himself around in his overstuffed black desk chair. He glanced at the phone, wishing for a case.

He stopped spinning and faced the full-length mirror that hung on the wall facing him. If nothing came through today, he might go out again tonight. He liked women and women liked his looks, well most women he had to admit. For some reason, he just couldn't fathom why Jasmine was immune to his charms.

He stared at himself. Blond hair, blue eyes, perfect teeth, and buff body with six pack abs. He liked keeping himself physically fit. He lifted a hand to run it through his hair but stopped, "I can't ruin perfection." It took him a half an hour just to get it looking like Chris Pines. The phone rang taking his attention from his reflection. He picked up the receiver, "Cross Paranormal Investigations."

"I'm Mayor Martin Westermann, and we're having a big paranormal problem here in Westilville, Missouri."

Spencer entered the towns name into his computer and brought it up on his computer. "I can get my team together today," he glanced at the clock on the wall. "But it's a little late for us to head your way. My team and I can be there sometime tomorrow." His lips curved up in a smile. "Don't worry, sir, my team will do everything they can to solve your problem."

"That would be great, we really need assistance. The Sheriff's department is at their wits end with these calls, and your team came highly recommended."

Spencer nodded, "My team takes paranormal problems seriously."

"I'll leave word with my clerk to expect you sometime tomorrow at the city hall, I'll be in my office until six pm."

"Just one other thing, one of my team members has a dog that travels with us. It helps us locate spirits."

"I'll let the clerk know. Thank you."

"You're welcome," Spencer replied as he hung up the phone, and started making phone calls to the other team members. As he hung up from the last call, his cell phone rang.

He picked it up and saw it was his mother, again. "Hey, mom."

"Are you coming over for dinner?"

"No, I can't. I've got a case, and the guys are coming over."

His mother sighed on the other end of the call, "Why can't you give up that ghost hunting? It doesn't pay anything. Why can't you be a nice boy and find a nice girl to marry. You know I'm not getting any younger."

He listened a little longer and then rolled his eyes as his mother continued to nag. When she paused to take a breath, he had his chance to get a word in. "I haven't found anyone I'm really interested in," as an image of Jasmine flashed in his mind. His doorbell rang. "Look, mom, I have to go. My team is arriving." He hung up before his mom could say anything else. "What a bore." He stepped out of his private office and slipped through the hall between the laundry room and the spare bedroom.

As he stepped into the living room, his feet sank down in the plush pile of the tan carpet. He opened the white door with beveled glass and stepped back to allow Fred Krieger and Roland Freed to enter. They were sort of opposites of the same coin.

Fred was short and muscular while Roland was tall and thin. Fred was dark haired with gray eyes, and Roland had brown hair and greenish brown eyes. They were best friends since high school who referred to each other as a brother from another mother. Roland grinned as he entered the house, "Sampson's picking up Jasmine and Bella, and they'll be here soon."

Spencer closed the door keeping the stifling heat outside and strode over to the overstuffed leather couch and let himself drop onto a cushion. "I sort of wish she'd get rid of that dog," He figured without the dog he'd be able to get her into bed with him. Then she'd know he was the man for her.

Fred shook his head then he and Roland shared a knowing look, they both knew why he didn't want the dog around. They weren't stupid and knew why Jasmine didn't care for Spencer, it was his personality.

Spencer sighed, and examined his fingernails, "I was just kidding."

Roland walked towards the kitchen, "You got anything to eat?" Roland seemed to always be hungry, yet the man never put on a pound.

Spencer leaned forward, pulled out his wallet, pulled out his credit card, and passed it over to Roland. "Why don't you just call for pizza or something. I'll pay for it."

Fred dropped onto a chair that matched the couch, "So, what's the case?"

"I'll wait until Devin and Jasmine get here. We'll need some information on the town we'll be heading to. The equipment needs to be loaded into one of the two Escapes. We'll be taking both."

Fred snorted, "You always say we'll wait, and then you tell us anyway."

The two men in the living room could hear Roland putting in the order but couldn't make out what he was saying. Roland stepped back into the room and passed the card back to Spencer.

They heard a knock on the door, "I'll get it," Roland said as he crossed the room to the door and pulled it open. Devin Sampson entered followed by the dog in question Bella who's back reached their knees.

Jasmine followed strawberry blond hair was done up in a bun on the top of her head. Her makeup brought out brown eyes, dressed in a pair of skinny black jeans, motorcycle boots, stretchy top with white spaghetti straps.

Spencer usually liked his women with more on the chest, but he could make allowances. Besides her caramel skin gave her an exotic appearance.

Devin glanced around the room, "What's up?"

Spencer gazed at Devin, "We can wait until the food arrives."

Jasmine didn't need to use her psychic abilities to read Spencer. He was just a teensy bit agitated as he drummed his fingers on the couch arm. "I guess your mom called again."

He pointed at her and clicked his thumb and mouthed boom at the same time as if he was firing a gun.

"And let me guess, she wanted you to come to dinner too," she said as she stood by the door. Her boots making depressions in the carpet where she stood.

"Yeah, but I told her I couldn't because all of you were coming over."

Jasmine shook her head. Why should it surprise her? He was such a big goof using them as an excuse. "She lives next door. Both your mom and dad were pressed against the window watching us. Creepy."

He shuddered as he said, "They have this idea that at twenty-nine I should be married and giving them grandchildren. Kids are scary."

Jasmine turned away and put a hand over her mouth to try to not to laugh, but her shaking body was a dead giveaway. She stopped took a breath, wiped a tear from her eye, and turned around to face him. "I don't know why you're not married yet..." she shrugged her shoulders. "Both Fred and Roland are while Devin's got his steady girlfriend," she eyed Spencer but had no interest in continuing the conversation.

She walked into the kitchen. Jasmine knew Spencer. He wouldn't demean himself to get the dishes, so she got them and set the table in the dining room. It was unusual for Spencer to call them to his house They usually met at a fast food place. Bella pranced along behind her.

She walked back into the kitchen and pulled out some glasses and carried them back into the dining room placing them on the mahogany table. She'd been in the house a few times before when Spencer didn't want to do the fast food thing. Jasmine shook her head, the man made no sense. She heard the doorbell ring and then muffled voices, and then Bella pranced back and forth on her feet as her tongue dropped out of her mouth at the appetizing smell of food.

Roland carried a huge bag into the dining room and pulled out a bucket of chicken, mashed potatoes, and gravy, green beans, biscuits. He turned to the refrigerator and rooted around bringing out a pitcher of tea. "Let's eat," he called out loud enough to be heard in the living room as he carried the pitcher into the dining room and pulled out a chair from the table.

Jasmine did likewise, and she and Roland began spooning food on their plates before the others join them. "Any idea what this case is about?" she asked as she pulled out a chicken breast.

Roland shook his brown bangs out of his eyes, "Nope, for once he hasn't spilled the beans."

She pulled off a piece of meat from the chicken breast and fed it to Bella, "Isn't that interesting."

Spencer, Fred, and Devin trooped in from the living room. Each taking their seats and filling plates.

Jasmine took a bite of chicken and chewed, swallowing she gazed at Spencer. "So, what's the case."

"I got a call from the Mayor from Westilville, Missouri. Seems they have an extensive paranormal problem. He wouldn't go into details, but I want to get ready to leave here at the earliest tomorrow." He shoved a forkful of green beans into his mouth, chewed and washed it down with a gulp of tea. "We're going to take both of the Escapes," he shifted in his chair as his gaze locked onto Devin. "Dig up all information on Westilville. I want to know the town's history before we get there."

"No problem, I can do that," Devin said between forkfuls of mashed potatoes and green beans. His shoulder-length flaming red hair pulled back in a ponytail.

"We need to take every bit of equipment we have. When we get to Westilville tomorrow, we'll be meeting up with the mayor at city hall. So, Devin, you'll be riding with Jasmine and me, and Roland and Fred will take the other Escape."

Jasmine glared at the blond, "You never cease to amaze me with how often you say you want to work with me. But by the time we get there I'm ready to kill you."

He gazed back at her as his face twisted into a smirk. "Live with it." He put his hand up near his mouth and muttered under his breath, "I have to put up with your dog."

Jasmine passed more of her chicken to Bella who sat under the table. She finished her food, and stood up and rinsed her dishes, opened the dishwasher and stuffed them inside. "I need a ride back to my apartment, so I can pack my stuff."

Spencer gazed at her, "Be ready to leave by six tomorrow morning."

Devin stood up and rinsed out his dishes and followed Jasmine and Bella.

Chapter 2

Jasmine rushed out of her apartment with Bella on her heels. She locked her door and raced down the stairs from the second floor to the first floor. She was lucky that her apartment was by the outside stairwell.

Bella sensing Jasmine's excitement let out a woof. Jasmine had clothes and other items packed away in a carry-on bag, slung on her shoulder and another bag that held her laptop she carried in her hand. And strapped to Bella were bags that looked like motorcycle saddlebags that carried her paraphernalia for ghost hunting.

Jasmine pulled open the passenger rear side door, and Bella jumped in. She passed her carry-on bag and laptop to Devin who placed it with his and Spencer's luggage. She closed the door. Pulling open the passenger side door she climbed into the seat next to Spencer. She closed the door and pulled her seatbelt across her body.

Spencer gunned the Escape, and both black colored vehicles pulled out of the apartment buildings parking lot merging with traffic and heading for I-55 that would take them to Westilville, Missouri. He only gave her a glance when she climbed into the Ford Escape, hoping she'd approve of his latest coif.

Jasmine didn't even look his way after sitting down in the seat. They both heard keys clicking in the backseat. Devin was using his laptop to look up information on the town they were traveling to.

After several minutes of searching, Devin cleared his throat to make sure they were listening to him. He heard the beep which meant that Spencer had opened the two-way communications between the SUV's. "Can everyone hear me okay?"

"Coming through loud and clear," Fred's voice came over the internal speaker system of the first vehicle.

"Westilville has a population of about three thousand. It's surrounded by forest to the south-west and farms around the north and west ends of town. Westilville was founded around the same time as Perryville, Missouri by Elijah Wilson who resented Commodore Perry. He named the town Westilville because it was the westernmost town in Perry County at that time.

"The French first settled Perry county in 1673. At the end of the French and Indian War, the land was handed over to the Spanish. The Osage Indians were a constant threat to the west even though they traded with the Europeans at times. But didn't like the Europeans hunting on their hunting grounds.

"The Spanish invited the Shawnee and Delaware tribes to come in and settle certain areas of Perry County. It was sort of a brilliant idea because it created a buffer between the Osage and the Europeans."

Jasmine glanced over at Spencer. "Conflicts might have happened that were never recorded in the history books. This could be a source of some of the paranormal activity."

Spencer at first didn't say anything as he continued to drive, but he glanced at her out of the corner of his eye. "We'll see."

Jasmine blew out a breath and crossed her arms across her chest. The man could be infuriating at times. Other times he could almost, almost be decent.

Devin took a sip of his bottle of water before beginning his run down again. "In 1795 the Spanish handed out land grants like candy. Over one hundred grants were issued with about forty-one going to people from Kentucky.

"The Spanish secretly sold the land back to France who then sold it to the US in the Louisiana Purchase to fund Napoleon's latest war. Afterward, more Americans and Europeans settled the land. In 1821 Perry county was officially organized and named on May 21, 1821."

"Anything else we should know," Fred's voice came over the speakers.

"No, there's nothing else. We'll have to talk to the mayor to find out who's being haunted, then we can look up that information."

Jasmine nodded, she glanced down at her watch. A couple more hours to go and they'd be in Westilville she hoped.

Jasmine watched the scenery pass by. Breakfast had been a very simple affair of a couple of pieces of toast. Her stomach felt hollow as she glanced at a sign and heard Bella whine. "We need to stop. Bella needs a pit stop."

Spencer glanced her way. "Now? "We've only got twenty-five miles to go."

She glanced down at her watch it read ten thirty. "Yes now."

Spencer hit his turn signal to let the guys in the identical Ford Escape know they were pulling off at the rest stop. They pulled in followed the sign over to the area designated for cars and pickup trucks. He pulled into the spot.

Jasmine hopped out of the Escape and opened the rear passenger door letting Bella out. She snapped the leash to Bella's collar and led her over to the grass so the dog could sniff the ground and circled a few times before she finally squatted and did her business.

Jasmine led her back to the Escape, and she took off the leash and let Bella into the vehicle. "I've got to go myself, does anyone needs anything while I'm in there?"

Fred and Roland each passed her some money. "Two Cokes."

Jasmine looked at Devin and Spencer, neither said anything. She shrugged her shoulders and rushed down the sidewalk toward the small concrete building. She hurried into the restroom and quickly made use of the facilities.

She washed her hands and stepped out into the area that had a map of Missouri and showing her where she was and a few of the other towns in the area. She stepped over to the Coke machine and bought two Cokes, and then herself a Sprite.

Her stomach rumbled, so she stepped over to a vending machine and picked out a bag of Chili Cheese Fritos. She dropped her coins into the machine and pressed the button. The bag fell, she pulled them out of the machine and walked back to the twin Ford Escapes.

Jasmine passed over Fred and Roland's drinks, then she climbed back into the vehicle she was riding in, and pulled open the bag of chips and twisted the cap off the bottle of Sprite and took a sip.

Spencer frowned at her, turned the key in the ignition and then backed out of the lot and headed back to the interstate. The other SUV followed along.

They continued to drive in silence as Jasmine ate her chips and drank the sprite. Spencer turned his head towards her once and glared. Devin patted Bella on the head as she laid in the seat beside him. The only sounds were of Jasmine crunching chips and drinking the Sprite.

Devin would have liked to listen to the radio, but he needed to stay available to look up anything else Spencer might want. The man always did this, and it was nerve rattling. But Jasmine could give as good as she got, and

Devin figured this was equal to a shot across the bow since she wasn't talking.

Twenty-five miles later they exited off I-55 and merged onto Lorimer Parkway which led straight into the town. They passed a McDonald's, Cracker Barrel, and a motel and hit the light at Main Street.

They turned down Main Street and passed a bunch of businesses that seemed to be usual in any small town. They found the circle in the middle of town and pulled into the circle and then in the lot behind city hall.

It was a two-story building that sat in between the library and the post office. On the other side of the circle were three other buildings which housed the sheriff's office, jail, and courthouse. All the buildings were encased in sandstone. The state and US. Flags sat off to the side in-between both sets of buildings. In the center of the circle sat a park with several trees. It wasn't large, but it wasn't small either.

The entire team climbed out of the vehicles and locked them up tight. Jasmine hooked Bella up to a leash. She was glad to be out of the vehicle and pranced beside Jasmine as they walked out from behind the buildings and walked into city hall.

The man sitting behind the desk glared at the dog. "You can't come in here with that animal."

Spencer stepped forward, "I'm Spencer Cross of Cross Paranormal Investigations, and this is my team. Mayor Westermann said he'd notify you that we were coming with a dog."

The man sighed as if he was a deflating balloon. Jasmine could only guess that he didn't get his daily dose of ruining someone's day yet. "So, he did," he said as he pointed over at the door. "You'll find the mayor and Sheriff Joshua Delmont in there."

Spencer led the group over to the door where he stuck his head in, "Mayor Westermann?" He looked in to see a man behind the desk who was about fifty pounds overweight with male pattern baldness wearing an off the rack dress suit. The sheriff wore a khaki shirt and brown slacks. The badge on his chest announced his profession while the webbed utility belt held the tools of his trade.

Westermann looked up from his desk and then stood. "Spencer Cross? You're younger than I thought you'd be."

Spencer smiled, "I get that all the time. This is my team," he made the introductions. "We'd like to get right to work if you don't mind."

The mayor gave Spencer his full attention though he appeared to be distracted. "No, no, of course not. Take a seat," his eyes roved over the group, but they stopped on Bella. "What an unusual looking dog."

A small smile pulled at Jasmine's mouth. "This is Bella, she's a Greater Swiss Mountain dog. She warns me if there's a dangerous entity around that I don't sense first. She's very useful to us."

"Smart dog," the mayor smiled back. He pulled a file off the top of the pile and passed it over to Spencer. "We had a strange incident that happened about three days ago. John and Ashley Schmidt, live in the Appleton Lane, Apartments. They have a ten-year-old son, Trevor, who's autistic. Trevor for his disability is very bright even though he's non-verbal. He went missing for two days. His trail led us into the forest, but something frightened him. His parents report he is now having nightmares. They are in dire need of help."

Spencer opened the file and turned his gaze back onto the mayor. "I haven't taken on a case like this, sounds interesting."

Jasmine snorted but kept her mouth shut for the time being.

Sheriff Delmont glared at the team of ghost hunters. "Just to let you know, I don't believe in ghosts or anything that goes bump in the night. I think you all are full of crap, so stay out of my way," his eyes hard as he stormed out of the office.

Mayor Westermann shook his head. The light glinting off the top of his head that shown through the thinning hair. "Sorry about that, but the Sheriff he doesn't believe. I'm keeping an open mind about this. When you're finished with that one, I have about six more for you."

Spencer rose from his chair and shook the mayor's hand, and the ghost hunters stepped out of city hall and into the sunlight. He turned to Jasmine. "What was that about inside the mayor's office?"

Jasmine smiled back, "Oh, I remembered the last case we worked on. You got so scared you ran. Man, I swear you'd put Freddy Jones from Scooby Doo to shame. You went screaming like a girl."

His blue eyes narrowed, but then he threw his head up high. Misdirection would be the safest way to go right now to save face in front of the male members of the team. "I didn't go screaming like a girl. I ran to put you to the test to see if you knew what you were talking about. I want all of my team to be experts in this field."

Roland grinned and threw his arm over Spencer's shoulders. "You'd do better if you circled the wagons," then burst out laughing.

Spencer shook his head at Roland's comment. "Let's take a trip over to Appleton Lane. I think we passed it on the way here."

The team of ghost hunters walked back to their vehicles and loaded up. They pulled out of the parking lot, drove around the circle to exit on State Street, and turned right. The SUV's passed through two traffic signals before they were stopped at a four-way stop and waited for their turn then hung a left onto Appleton Lane. They pulled into the parking lot, and they climbed out of their vehicles. Spencer stopped for a moment. "I don't want to overwhelm these people."

Jasmine nodded, "Actually, it's best not to overwhelm Trevor. Autistic people can become overwhelmed by too much going on around them."

"Okay, Fred, Roland, and Devin, why don't you guys go and check us into the motel down on Lorimer while me and Jasmine talk to the family."

Small towns mystified Jasmine, but this one looked pretty self-sufficient. Usually, they relied on big business to keep them up and running, but with all the small family run businesses and the several corporate ones in town the people seemed like they were doing fine.

Jasmine and Spencer climbed the stairs of the long red brick building and walked down the balcony to apartment 12 B. Spencer knocked on the red door. Bella stood between them on her leash.

The door opened, and a woman peeked out at them. She wore her short auburn hair cut in a bob and wore a yellow shirt paired with yellow slacks and house shoes. The most noticeable thing about her was the dark circles under her eyes. "Can I help you?"

"Ashley Schmidt?"

"Yes?"

"I'm Spencer Cross of Cross Paranormal Investigations, and this is Jasmine Stone and her dog Bella. We'd like to come in and talk to you about Trevor and his experience."

Her tired eyes lit up a bit, "Yes, yes, please come in. Mayor Westermann called and said you were coming," she opened the door wider to allow them to enter.

"Where's a good spot to set up?" Spencer asked as he glanced around the quaintly decorated living room which consisted of a blue overstuffed couch and a recliner facing a TV with a squat wooden coffee table, small end table with a lamp sitting on it, and one of the tall standing floor lamps in the corner. Brown worn carpet covered the floor.

"Is your husband home?" Jasmine asked.

"No, he works as the store manager of the McDonald's," she glanced at the clock the hands told her it was twelve thirty pm. "He won't be home until five this evening, but he told Trevor this morning that he'd bring him home some chicken nuggets and a hot fudge sundae if Trevor was a good boy." She smiled at the pair of investigators, but her eyes blinked rapidly and she bit her bottom lip as she glanced at Bella.

Jasmine sensed the other woman's nervousness and smiled gently. "Don't worry, Bella has never harmed anyone. She's a good girl," Jasmine said as she pet the dog's head

That seemed to put Mrs. Schmidt more at ease. Spencer leaned forward on the couch. "Can you tell us what happened to Trevor?"

"I had to work, and I called Mrs. Johnson who lives two doors down to see if her daughter Darla could watch Trevor when he got home from school. Mrs. Johnson has a key to the apartment, and she said Darla would love to watch Trevor." They heard a sudden spate of what sounded like a sing-song voice coming from one of the other rooms, but it sounded more like baby babble.

"That's Trevor, I kept him home from school today. He's not sleeping through the night, so I get up and try to coax him to go back to sleep by getting in the bed with him. He seems to be afraid of something. It's like he's looking at something in the corner of his room.

"But back to your original question. Darla came over to watch Trevor, but she didn't do so great of a job because when I got home the door was open and Darla was in the kitchen with a friend playing on their cell phones. I couldn't find Trevor anywhere. I called the Sheriff's office, and they set off looking for him. They say he went into the woods, but they didn't find him in the woods. They found him by Park Drive Cemetery."

Jasmine wondered if this was significant. "Where is that located?"

Tears glittered in the woman's eyes, and she sniffed as her hands trembled. "The other end of town. I know you aren't around here, but he had to cross several streets to get there. I just don't understand why he was there or what could have happened to him."

At that moment Trevor ran into the room. He wore a blue and gray striped shirt, jeans, and tennis shoes. He had short brown hair, blue eyes with some brown flecks in the blue. He smiled at them then baby babbled at the dog, and stepped over to Bella. He gazed into Bella's eyes and then reached out to stroke her head, and then he hugged the dog and made noises.

Jasmine smiled, but then she stopped. Images flashed in her mind. An ugly woman, a spectral hound with red eyes, someone running, and then a man in darkness. Jasmine shook her head. The man kept flashing in her mind.

Ashley glanced at the younger woman. "Are you okay?"

Jasmine brought a hand up to her head and rubbed at her forehead. "I believe Trevor is projecting his memories to me," she squeezed her eyes and managed to erect her mental barrier before she was overwhelmed. "Didn't mean to scare anyone, but I wasn't prepared for that."

Spencer turned off his mini-voice recorder. He'd listen to the playback later. "Do you think it might be possible if we come back to perform a night investigation?"

"I'd have to talk to John about it, but I believe he'd agree if it means that Trevor's nightmares stop."

Spencer pulled a card out of his pocket and passed it over to Ashley. "If he says yes contact me on my cell phone. We're going to be in town for a while."

Trevor stood up and jabbered once more then he started laughing and jumped up and down moving in a circle. He ran off back to his room and slammed the door.

Ashley laughed as she saw her guests to the door. "It's time for his nap," she explained to the pair of ghost hunters as they exited the apartment.

As they approached the Ford Escape now out of hearing distance from the apartment, Spencer turned to Jasmine, "You want to explain what happened back there?"

"It's hard to explain, but when Trevor hugged Bella, I was flooded with images that just don't make any sense to me." They descended the stairs, and Jasmine leaned against the Escape. She brought her hands up to her eyes, "I don't feel so good."

Spencer unlocked the Escape and hopped into the driver's seat, "You just probably need something to eat."

Jasmine opened the rear passenger door and got Bella in the Escape, and she closed the door. She hopped into the passenger side and closed the door. She closed her eyes and saw the man again behind her eyelids. "Who are you," she whispered.

Spencer pulled the SUV out into traffic and headed for the motel. "What are you muttering about?"

Jasmine glanced back at Bella, she wasn't acting unusual which told her it wasn't bad whatever was going on with her. She grimaced as a stab of pain hit her in the left eye socket next to her nose. "Nothing," but she felt like something, or someone was trying to contact her.

Silence filled the Escape as Spencer drove to the Motel. They climbed out of the vehicle and Jasmine got Bella out of the SUV, and they entered. Spencer stepped up to the clerk and received two room keys from the clerk. He passed one over to Jasmine.

Spencer handed her an electronic key card with the magnetic strip. "You're in room twenty-five," as he reluctantly released the card.

Jasmine swayed like a drunk as she walked over to the SUV and pulled her stuff from the back of the vehicle. "I'm going to go and lie down for a while." Rest she needed rest she told herself. She walked to her room, still swaying from the pain in her head.

Spencer kept an eye on her as she walked over to her motel room. He needed to make sure she got inside without any problems.

Chapter 3

Jasmine entered her room with Bella at her side and unhooked the leash from the dog's collar. Bella sniffed around the room and huffed. "If that means you don't like the accommodations then I'm in perfect agreement."

She closed the door, and locked the two deadbolts and slid the chain into place on the door. That didn't exactly make her feel all that safe. She sat her laptop bag and carry on bag on the small round table over by the smudged window. She pulled the curtain closed blocking out most of the light.

A TV hung secured to the wall, but she didn't want to watch it, all she wanted was rest that she promised herself she needed. She sat on the full-sized bed and sighed as the springs squeaked. She looked up at the ceiling, "Figures." She pulled her battered motorcycle boots off and lay down on the bed.

Even though she could hear doors from other rooms opening and closing, cars starting out in the parking lot, voices, and traffic from the street she slipped into a deep sleep.

Jasmine opened her eyes, and she found herself standing in the dark. She looked around as her eyes became adjusted to the darkness. "I must be dreaming." A movement out of her peripheral vision drew her attention a little crack where light flowed in. What she could see looked like a cave. She tried to stay calm, but her body trembled. Her heart raced, thumping hard in her chest. "Hello, is anyone there?"

Biting her bottom lip her senses tingle, someone or something was out there in the dark with her. Images of creatures ran through her mind until she couldn't take it anymore and yelled at the top of her lungs, "Show yourself!"

Something brown moved into the light. She took a step back away from it and stumbled over a rock as the palms of her hands were clammy and cold. She rubbed them over her jean covered thighs. Then she saw the fringe. It was a buckskin shirt.

A voice came out of the darkness, "I did not mean to frighten you."

She brought her hands up, she'd taken a self-defense class but didn't realize she'd need to put the teaching to use. But she can tell this person means her no harm as her arms fall back down to her sides. "Who are you?"

"Everit Black, at your service," he said by way of introduction. His voice was little gravely but pleasant to listen to. It was like he hadn't used it in a while.

She glanced around, and it hit her just like a punch right between the eyes. This is the man from Trevor's mental images. "You've been trying to contact me, why?"

"I connected with Trevor, and I saw you through his eyes and just knew you'd be able to help me," he paused. His movements were careful and slow not wanting to frighten her again. "You see I've been trapped here for a very long time and you're the only one I feel I can trust."

She frowned but looked away trying to avoid direct eye contact. "I need more information."

He sat on a rock. Light shining on his brown skin a copper color. His long very dark black hair hung down to maybe his waist. His high cheekbones indicated to her his ancestry was Native American, dark eyes straight nose, and full lips. He took a deep breath and held up his hands.

"I have lived a long time. I loved many women, and had many children, but," he paused in his narration. "I seem to be cursed." He knew he wasn't telling her the whole truth. If he did, it might frighten her, and he didn't want that. "I don't seem to grow old in the normal sense of nature. I have never been able to find out why. But when the women I was with started questioning why I didn't grow older I would disappear and make it appear as if I died, I know it was not a good thing to do by leaving the women to raise our children. But I knew they would be taken care of."

Jasmine crossed her arms over her chest and pursed her lips together. Somewhere deep inside she wanted to believe his story, but she found herself not sure if she could believe this far-fetched story. But, she questioned herself, how could she explain his clothing. "How did you come to be trapped?"

"I started over anew. I married a Shawnee woman, and I became a trapper," he pulled at the buckskin sleeve covered with long fringe on the underside of the sleeve. "I was on my way back to our village but found this cave to provide shelter in a storm. But my haven turned out to be my cell when the ground started shaking. I tried to get out but the opening closed. I remembered a story told by a friend on how to survive which was to put myself into the sleep of death.

"So, I did what he told me until three days ago when I was awakened by Trevor. His fear was great, and it pulled me from my sleep. I've been trying to dig myself out of here and have made some progress but not much." He cocked his head as he stared at her, "You don't believe me?"

"Let's just say I'm skeptical."

"Sorry but I don't know what skep-skeptical means."

"It means I don't know if you're telling me the truth or not," she said.

He stood from his seat and moved forward towards her.

Jasmine moved back a step as her mouth went dry and her muscles tensed. "Don't come near me!" Her mind flew in a million directions as she worried at who or what he might be.

"Don't fear. I won't harm you. I just need to connect to our minds. I don't know why, but you are my guiding light," he said as he touched her temple.

She flinched at his touch as a spark like electricity flared between them and the last she knew she felt his arms catch her as she collapsed and her eyes rolled up in the back of her head. She jerked and opened her eyes to find herself back in the hotel room with the light from the sun beaming straight into her eyes through the crack in the curtain as the sun began to set.

Bella whined as the dog lay next to her. "I'm sorry, Bella, I'll take you out for a walk," Jasmine said as rose and sat on the corner of the bed and tugged on her motorcycle boots. She grabbed Bella's discarded leash and picked up the electronic key card off the table. Unlocking the two deadbolts and sliding the chain from the door she opened the door and stepped outside to the cooler temperature.

She led Bella off into the grass that ran in between motel buildings. As they walked, her mind kept coming back to Everit Black. What was he? Who was he? He could pass for a full-blood Cherokee which made up part of her heritage.

Jasmine and Bella walked around the back of the second building and then stepped out in between the third building and headed back to her room. Feeling hungry, and knowing Bella probably was she'd decided to look and see if there was a pizza place around that would deliver to the motel.

She hurried back to her room. She couldn't help it, she felt like she was being watched. She glanced over her shoulder to see a man standing by a white car with a yellow stripe down the side. He gave her the creeps as she fumbled with her key card but finally got her door open. She and Bella stepped inside, and she quickly threw the deadbolts and slid the chain over the door.

Pulling out her laptop, she drew out her private router with her own VPN settings and connected the router to the laptop and plugged the router in. She quickly checked her bank account. Then checked out the options for food delivery in Westilville and decided on a pizza.

Finally, she went to Google, and in the search engine, she typed in the name Everit Black trapper. She didn't expect to find anything when Google finally came up with a drawing and a sort of footnote that stated that Everit Black disappeared seemingly off the face of the earth during the series of earthquakes of 1811and 1812 caused by the New Madrid Faultline.

She sat back in the chair. It creaked as she leaned into the chair back. In a way, she couldn't believe that the story he told was true, but somewhere inside she was glad that it was true. She stopped and stared at the wall as her mouth dropped open. "No way," she said to herself. That would make him over two hundred and five years old.

She tried to shake the feeling that someone was watching her, so she pulled out her cell phone. Seeing no calls, she punched in Spencer's number. "Hey," she said into the phone as he answered. "Did the Schmidt's agree to a home investigation?"

"Yes, they did. We're going over there at ten tonight, they're going to go to his parents' house."

"Okay, I'll be ready," she replied as she hung up the cell phone. She turned to Bella, "I'm going to take a quick shower," she said as she dug into her overnight bag and pulled out a blue and white tank top and a pair of blue jeans, and some underwear.

She pulled out her shampoo and soap and stepped into the bathroom and turned on the shower. She waited five minutes for the water to warm and stepped into the lukewarm stream. "Better than nothing," she said as she ducked her head under the water and poured shampoo in her hand and rubbed it into her hair. She scrubbed her scalp and waited for a second and then ducked her head back under the water.

Jasmine quickly soaped up, but the water never got above lukewarm. She rinsed off and then turned the water off, and dried off with the thin, rough towels. She stepped out into the main room and quickly dressed. She had this feeling she was being watched, but she heard a knock on the door, and answered it, paid the driver, and carried the pizza, and a coke that she had ordered over to the table.

Bella barked in excitement, and her tongue lolled out of her mouth in anticipation of food. Jasmine pulled the lid off the medium-sized pizza box and pulled off a piece for Bella. "Be careful, it's hot," she said as she pulled another piece off and bit into the cheesy goodness. The crust was a little well done, but other than that it was fine in her opinion.

As she ate, she signed into her website and checked the status of her sales. Two more sales made. She emailed her sister with the details on who to ship the jewelry too. Jasmine made enough money with her business she could hire her sister to be the shipping clerk.

Jasmine ate two more pieces, and then looked down at Belle who whined at her. "Sorry girl, but one piece is your limit. You'll have to finish up with your food." She pulled out a small bag of dry dog food and a two-sectioned dog dish. She walked into the bathroom and poured water on one side and then put food on the other side.

Bella tried using those big brown eyes of hers to get another piece of pizza. "Sorry girl, but if I give you any more, you'll get fat." She knelt and put the dish down in front of the dog. Then she grabbed her by the head and ruffled the fur on the sides of her dog's cheeks.

She stood, closed the laptop, and unhooked everything putting it away. She picked up her watch and slipped the band over her hand and fit it onto her wrist. She glanced at her watch seven thirty. She had at least two hours to kill. She stepped into the bathroom and brushed her Strawberry blond hair back and pulled it into a ponytail.

She pulled out her saddlebags and pulled out the items she had stuffed into them before leaving her home that morning. She wasn't sure what she might need, so she picked out several items and put them into a smaller case that she carried with her on investigations.

She pulled out the long strap that allowed her to carry the smaller case about the size of a small messenger bag over her chest. She then propped herself up on the bed with Bella at her side while she flipped through the limited channels on the TV.

She allowed her mind to wander as Bella put her head in Jasmine's lap. She absentmindedly rubbed the dog's head. How could a man live over two hundred years, but if what he said was true he could be older than that.

She heard a door open near her room followed by footsteps approaching her room. They footsteps stopped outside and then a soft knock on the door. She rose and unlocked the door but left the chain in place as she pulled the door open enough to see who was on the other side of the door. Devin stood here, "Hey, Spencer says he wants to leave about nine thirty, so I thought I'd let you know so you can take Bella for a walk."

Bella upon hearing her name jumped off the bed with a thump and bumped Jasmine's knees knocking her human over so she could shove her nose into the opening of the door. She gave a soft woof and sniffed at the door.

"Hang on a sec, and we'll come out. She could use another walk to work off that piece of pizza she had earlier," Jasmine picked up the leash off the table and hooked it Bella's collar. She closed the door a bit to slide the chain off and then joined Devin.

"I took her in the grass behind the motel," she said. She didn't say anything about the man who was watching her earlier in the day, she was sure he was watching someone else and not her.

"Any idea of what to expect tonight?" Devin asked.

"I don't know. I think Trevor has some psychic ability, but it's hard to be sure since I can't question him he's non-verbal." They walked through the grass behind the first building letting Bella do her business.

Devin stopped and looked up at the thin clouds that drifted slowly across the sky as the continued to darken towards night. "Isn't that kind of dangerous?" he asked as he glanced over at her as a light breeze blew around them and played with their hair.

"It is, but I have a secret weapon to protect Trevor when we can't be around, and I'll give it to his mother," she said as she smiled.

"You're a bit mysterious tonight," Devin grinned back at her. "I guess we better get ready to leave or Spencer will be ready to bust a gut." They turned and walked out in front of the building to the parking lot where the twin Ford Escapes were parked.

As they stood there the rest of the team came out of their rooms to join them. Jasmine saw Spencer come out of the room next to hers. Now she was sure she knew who was spying on her earlier and her flesh crawled as she thought he might have had his eye pressed to the window peering in at her through the slit in the curtains.

Jasmine didn't say anything but pursed her lips then turned to Devin. "You can ride up front with him."

Spencer unlocked the vehicle, and Jasmine opened the door and put Bella in the back and then she climbed in behind her, and she slammed the door. She held her chin up and crossed her arms across her chest as the muscles of her body tightened. Pissed was a light word to use right now. Furious might be more like it, but she kept her silence.

Devin sighed as he sat in the front passenger seat wondering to himself what the man across from him had done to make her so mad this time. Whatever it was it was going to be a tense ride over to the Schmidt's.

Thankfully the drive was about ten minutes to the Schmidt's apartment building. They pulled into the parking lot and found a couple of places to park. As they climbed out of the vehicles, Fred called out, "Hey, Spencer, what kind of equipment do you want to take."

Spencer strolled over to Fred, "Let's take the EMF meters, a laser grid, rem pod, a couple of motion sensors, and a couple of cameras along with the IRL camera."

"You got it," Fred replied as he and Roland began to grab the pieces of equipment. Devin came over and helped them with the cable and the DVR and laptop they'd use for making the recordings.

"I don't know what's going on, but Jasmine totally clammed up when Spencer came around. She didn't say one word to him and told me to ride up front. I don't think he liked it."

Roland glanced around to make sure no one could overhear him. "I saw Jasmine briefly when they came back from the Schmidt's she didn't look good."

"You don't think he tried anything with her, do you?" Devin asked.

Fred chuckled, "No, I think if he tried she would have beat him to a pulp. Now let's get this stuff out of here before he comes back to see what's taking us so long."

Jasmine climbed out of the Escape with Bella in tow and saw the Schmidt's down by their car. "Mrs. Schmidt," she called out as she approached.

Ashley turned and then she smiled as Trevor jumped up and down excitedly next to her. "Calm down Trevor," she said to her son and then faced Jasmine. "John, this is one of the ghost hunters I was telling you about and her dog that Trevor is so fond of."

John stepped up and stuck his hand out. Jasmine took it, his grip was firm but not hard. "Mrs. Schmidt, I'm going to give you something now," she reached into her bag and pulled out a shiny black stone. "This is black tourmaline. It'll help keep Trevor safe, and he shouldn't be bothered by anything after we get through tonight. Place it somewhere in his room after you return where he can't find it."

Ashley grinned. "Yes, he is pretty sneaky at times."

John held out a key, "This is a spare key to the apartment. I'd appreciate it if you'd lock up after you're finished."

Jasmine nodded and smiled at the family and then returned to the group she worked with.

"What did you give her?" Spencer wanted to know.

Jasmine glared back at him, "If it's any of your business I gave her a piece of polished black tourmaline. It has properties that will help protect Trevor after we're done." She turned her back on him and stormed up the stairs towards the Schmidt's apartment.

"What's with her?" he asked to no one. He had a small idea that she might have caught him sneaking a peek at her through the gap in the curtains of her room. That was after he ran the other guy off.

Chapter 4

Jasmine entered the apartment before the guys could get there. She didn't want to be anywhere near Spencer. However just her luck Spencer followed with the other guys bringing up the rear.

"Set up the laser grid in Trevor's room," he said as he started handing out orders like a general getting ready to send his men into battle. "Make sure there's a camera near the laser grid. We want to get any evidence on film.

"Devin set up and man the DVR let me know if anything happens, no telling how long it will take to get any evidence." He turned to Fred as Roland followed Jasmine toward Trevor's room. "Set out the rem pod and two motion detectors." He picked up the IRL camera and set off to the room.

As the men finished setting things up, Bella growled. Jasmine took the leash off, "Seek." Bella walked off and headed into the boy's room sniffing around. Jasmine stopped and looked around. "I feel anger. Hatred."

She flinched and glanced around hoping no one saw her. She heard Everit in her mind, "I have to warn you, this spirit wants Trevor to die."

Her eyes grew as she whispered, "How do you know?" She wanted to give voice to how he was in her mind but didn't say anything else in case someone was close and listening to her.

"It was one of the things his mind imparted to me."

She stood with her feet planted, but her hip cocked to one side. She really wanted to see him again so she could yell, but instead, she whispered, "You could have told me sooner."

"What are you muttering about," Spencer asked as he walked up to join her.

She waved him off, "It's nothing."

As he turned on the IRL camera, a crash came from the kitchen. Fred dashed off to the kitchen, but he returned to the room. "That's strange he said, it sounded like glass breaking.

The room temperature began to drop, and something cold touched the back of Jasmine's neck, but it grew white-hot, and she slapped a hand to the back of her neck as she grunted in pain, "Ow."

"What is it," Everit demanded to know.

Roland was at her side and brushed her ponytail away. "You've been scratched."

Jasmine looked around giving voice to what the others were thinking. "It's unusual for this much activity so soon."

The energy in the hall became more heavy and oppressive as Jasmine stepped inside Trevor's room. Her breathing became labored as though she couldn't breathe. She swallowed hard pushing her growing fear back.

Bella starts growling as she stood at a corner by the head of the bed. The hair on her back bristles as her barks become loud, urgent. The rem pod starts beeping as something is in the corner blocking out some of the lights of the laser grid. The EMF meters start going berserk with an insistent whining and buzzing that lowers in volume then rises in volume.

Spencer says loudly, "Who are you? What do you want?"

A woman's voice responds but loud enough for everyone to hear, "DIE!"

"NO!" Jasmine responds to the voice. "You will not harm us, and YOU WILL NOT HARM TREVOR!" She dug into her case at her side and pulled out a bundle of sage and abalone shell along with a bottle of holy water.

Her stomach twisted as if something reached inside her and twisted her insides. The wind whipped up. Jasmine grunted again in pain, "She's really pissed off, and she's trying to stop me." She turned toward the corner where Bella stood. "You won't stop me. Do you hear me? You won't stop me." She pulled out a lighter, flicked the flame on, and lit the bundle.

The continued to grow in intensity, but once the sage started to smolder she placed the stick into the abalone shell and put it in the corner. "Bella, come here." The dog moved over to her side and trembled as she continued to growl and bark.

She picked up the holy water and began to chant a Cherokee blessing. She splashed the holy water into the corner and steps in to draw the sign of the cross on the walls.

The wind stopped as suddenly as it started. The cold pain in her abdomen is no longer there. The room felt lighter, "She's gone." Jasmine turned to Spencer. "I guess I owe you an explanation. I will only tell you this, if you ever spy on me again while I'm getting undressed in my room, I'll personally punch you out. Got it!" She collected the items she'd pulled out of her bag, then put herself into his face invading his personal space. "Do I make myself clear?"

Now waiting for an answer, she took a couple of steps back and bent over and hooked Bella's leash to her collar. She tossed the apartment key to Spencer then stormed out of the apartment and led Bella down to the vehicles. She'd be damned if she stayed in the same room with that idiot.

The breeze blew, and she felt a sting at the back of her neck and touched her neck. She knew exactly what it was when she touched the wet, sticky warmth, blood. Not much there but the scratches were sensitive to the touch.

She glanced up at the night sky as the moon glowed behind some light clouds, she sniffed at the air and sighed. The rain was coming. She slowly calmed down, but inside she was still fuming, "How dare he," she mumbled.

At the same time, Fred glared at Spencer. His gray eyes flashing in anger, "Dammit did you have to piss her off?"

"It's not like I was the only the peeking through the window," He shrugged his shoulders like what he did wasn't that big of a deal. "I ran some guy off earlier," he grinned slightly, "Look, I'm a guy, and at least I did verify that's she's got a great body under those clothes."

Roland shook his head in disgust, "Dude, you're pathetic."

Devin silently agreed as they packed up the equipment.

As the men trooped out of the apartment, Spencer pulled the door shut behind him and locked the deadbolt.

He followed the other guys down the stairs to the vehicles. Fred unlocked the Escape that he was driving and Jasmine hopped into the back with Bella. She helped from the back seat to stow the equipment away.

Fred and Roland climbed into the vehicle, and they followed Spencer's down the road heading back toward the motel. At nearly one a.m. in the morning, there was very little to no traffic out on the streets.

Roland turned around in his seat, "Do you want to talk about it?"

"Not really," she started but changed her mind. She leaned forward, "You know, he wouldn't be so bad if he wasn't such a jerk all the time. I mean, he acts like such a jerk all the time! He's got this idea that he's god's gift to women, you know. But…" she stopped and glanced up at Fred. "There's also the incident when he yelled at me about the hoarder. Like I didn't know what the hell I was doing or that the woman's problem was all in her head."

"Well, I don't know about the god's gift to women thing, but I do know that's how he is. He's always been that way for as long as we've known him," Roland replied.

"What he's trying to say," Fred added, "is that we know how much of a jerk Spencer is. We've watched him stumble down this slippery slope before in high school," Fred he glanced up in the rearview mirror. "Once he knows it bothers you he'll do it again just to get a reaction out of you. It feeds his ego. Makes him feel like you want him."

Jasmine frowned, "As if." She couldn't help it as they pulled into the motel lot and parked when she yawned. "Sorry, but I'm wiped out. That took a lot out of me in the apartment, and I need sleep. I'll see you guys in the morning," she and Bella climbed out of the SUV and walked off to their motel room.

She opened the door, and Jasmine and the dog slipped into the room. She unhooked Bella's leash, locked the door, and then opened the pizza box and laid it on the floor giving her dog the last piece as a reward for being such a smart dog in the Schmidt's apartment.

Jasmine walked over to the bed stripped off her clothes and boots, pulled on an oversized T-shirt and laid down pulling the sheet over her. In minutes, she was asleep.

Jasmine opened her eyes and found herself in the dark place again. She sensed

Everit's presence near her. Hands grabbed her by the arms, and she found herself forced to sit on the rock where he had sat the last time they were together.

He pushed her head forward, not hard but not gently either. "What's your problem?" she tried to fight his hands off her.

"I asked you to be careful. I told you that she was dangerous and yet you still went ahead and confronted her," he reached into a pouch at his hip and pulled out a piece of cloth.

He gently dabbed it on the back of her neck. He pulled something else out of the pouch and rubbed the cool concoction into the scratches. "This will heal these up faster." He replaced the salve back into his pouch. He moved away from her.

She stood from the rock as her eyes grew accustomed to the dark. "Look," she stamped a foot in anger on the hard rock floor of the cave, "I couldn't allow her to stay there. You were the one who told me that she wanted to kill Trevor. Why?"

He shook his head, "I don't know. But remember this, she's dangerous."

"How do you know?"

Everit shrugged his shoulders, "I just know. I can feel it in my being. Now you have put yourself in her path. Take extra precautions, and remember this I will be with you."

"Why?"

A smile tugged at his full lips, "Because I don't like her. Anything that would try to hurt a harmless child needs to be destroyed," his dark eyes flashed.

"Well, she's gone from Trevor's room. I made sure of that plus I gave his mother a grounding stone. I believe he's got some psychic powers and the stone will keep all negative spirits from Trevor," Jasmine replied as she took a step toward him.

"You need to go back," Everit said as he cocked his head as if listening to something. He pulled her into a hug then kissed her on the forehead.

Jasmine's eyes closed and then they opened to find herself back in the motel room. She reached up to the back of her neck, the area of skin where she'd been scratched was now healed. "It worked," and she heard him chuckle in her mind.

She screwed her face up and realized someone was knocking on her door. She rose from her bed and unlocked the door and opened it a crack. "Yes?"

Roland stood out there on the walkway, "Spencer is paying for breakfast, he wants McDonald's, you want anything?"

"Egg McMuffin and coffee. Make it the largest size they have." After last night, she needed an extra boost to get her going.

Jasmine picked up the old pizza box off the floor and tossed it in the trash can. She pulled out a short sleeve T-Shirt and a pair of skinny jeans. She opened the curtain that hung over her window and glanced outside to see

Roland and Fred hopping into the SUV and backing out of the parking lot. She wondered if she had enough time to take a quick shower.

Turning on the water in the shower, she stripped down and hopped in. She didn't know what Everit was doing, but it seemed that communication with him through the psychic link he'd established with her only worked for her one way while his worked two ways.

It didn't seem quite fair she thought as she toweled off, and she knew these towels were a rip-off. As thin and rough that they were.

She pulled on her clothes as she wrapped her wet hair in a towel, and heard a knock on her door. When she opened it, Roland passed through her food. Bella smelling the food jumped off the bed and pranced over to Jasmine.

Jasmine giggled at the dog who sat down beside her chair and put her head on her human's thigh. "You are such a lush." Jasmine tore off a piece of the McMuffin and held it out.

Bella gingerly took the food from Jasmine's hand, and practically inhaled it, and looked up for more.

"Sorry girl, but mommas got to eat too," she couldn't help but wonder what Everit was eating.

Everit wasn't eating he was working and working hard to get out of this cave. He moved more rock out of the way. He heard movement outside the cave and stopped. He knew he had to be careful. He moved so he could look out through the slit in the rubble.

It was a couple of people who'd come to visit a grave in the cemetery. He closed his eyes and concentrated and very slowly drained just a fraction of their energy. He would need more.

He sat down on the rock and focused on Jasmine. He couldn't deny it, he was attracted to her but not only would there be a lot for him to learn he would have a lot to teach her too once she learned the truth. He kept hearing sounds and finally caught sight of a car. Strange, where was the horse?

He brought his focus back to the work at hand which was to get out of this cave. He felt he needed to be with Jasmine. If need be, he will protect her. He grabbed at another rock and moved it. An hour passed and sweat dripped from his brow. He pulled the buckskin shirt off, and his muscles rippled across his shoulders and chest as he pulled at more rocks.

Rock shifted, and the opening grew larger. He shoved at a rock by the opening and pushed it out of the way. More light illuminated his prison. He hoped that soon he would be free.

Chapter 5

Jasmine brushed her hair out, then she arranged the Strawberry blond hair into a messy bun on her head. She didn't like messing with it much. Her cell phone rang, and she raced out of the bathroom to the table. Picking it up she glanced at the caller ID and reluctantly answered.

Spencer's voice came through the speaker, "Get ready to go, we have a meeting with the mayor this morning."

"I need to walk Bella first," she said as she hung up on him without waiting for a reply.

She grabbed Bella's leash, attached it to her collar, and unlocked the door to her motel room. She stepped out and glanced up at the dark clouds hanging in the sky threatening rain. She stepped back into her room and grabbed her rain poncho out of her overnight bag. She carried it with her just in case.

Jasmine took Bella behind the building and let her do her business. As she and her dog came around the side of the building she heard the first splat of a big raindrop smacking onto the concrete. She raced over to the SUV's and got Bella in first and then she climbed in after. She wasn't afraid of getting wet, but she knew that if this turned into a thunderstorm, it could intensify the paranormal activity.

She didn't really notice which SUV she climbed into until she notices Spencer at the wheel. That's another thing that bugged

Jasmine is that Spencer didn't seem to trust anyone else with driving his precious vehicles, other than him and Fred.

He needed to get over it. She wanted something else to eat than fast food, and as they turned into the lot behind city hall, she saw a grocery store down the road. She'd make a mention of it when they left.

Jasmine also wanted to stop at the fruit market. She would need more food for Bella if this were going to be an extended stay. She wished there was a better place to stay than that cheapo' motel.

The SUV's parked and she pulled the rain poncho over her to keep her somewhat dry and then hopped out of the vehicle and led Bella out. She slammed the door a little harder than she meant and ducked her head to avoid Spencer's gaze. She took off at a run with her dog at her side.

The men took off running and reached the door before her. As they entered the building that housed city hall, Jasmine couldn't shake the feeling of being watched. She turned around, and on the other side of the circle, she saw the deputy watching her. A shudder ran through her body. She sensed that the deputy doesn't have good intentions.

She entered and tried to ignore his probing eyes and joined the others as they entered the mayor's office.

Mayor Westermann rose from his chair, a huge grin plastered on his jowly face as he stepped around his desk. The man was shorter than what she thought he was. He stuck his hand out to Spencer and pumped the younger man's hand, "Great job at the Schmidt's apartment. Both Ashley and John say the investigation was handled fantastically."

He released Spencer's hand and then took Jasmine's in his. "Ashley says she's grateful to you for the stone. She said Trevor is even happier than he was before."

Jasmine smiled, "That's great to hear."

Westermann turned back to Spencer, "That was just a test to see if your group knows what they're doing, and it looks like you all passed with flying colors." He picked up a file off his desk. "This is the Foley's house. Which is located on Carolina Street.

"Justin and Abigail Foley are in desperate need of help. They called me again this morning to see if you could come and investigate their house. They have two girls Laurel and Arlene. Abigail says Arlene is talking to what she thought was an imaginary friend, but she's not so sure anymore." He paused and gazed at the investigators.

"They called another paranormal team who came in and investigated but left after three hours and said they wouldn't be back. They left a recording with me," he lifted a DVD and handed it over to Spencer. "Whatever is going on in that house scared them so bad, they said they wouldn't come here again. I have high hopes that whatever is going on you'll figure it out."

"My team will do their best," Spencer said as he again shook the mayor's hand as the team walked out.

Devin turned to Spencer, "I'll see if the clerk can direct me to the town's records so I can try to find something about the history of the place."

"Good idea," Spencer clapped Devin on the shoulder. "While you're doing that we'll go back to the motel."

"Actually," Jasmine dared to butt in. "I want to go to the grocery and see what they have by way of food. I'm tired of fast food."

Spencer nodded, he was getting a little tired of it too. "I don't know what you can make at that motel."

"I saw a stove in the office, maybe the manager will let me use it," Jasmine replied.

"I'll see if he will. I brought a mini fridge with me that can hold anything that needs to be kept cold," Spencer grinned at the others. "Roland can ride back with Fred, and they can run you down there," he said as he pulled out a credit card and handed it to her. "Charge it on this, I can use it as a tax write off as a business expense."

She rolled her eyes as she took it, put Bella in the back of the SUV and they backed out of the parking place and headed down Main Street to the grocery store that sat on the corner of Jackson and State Street.

"Why do you and Spencer drive the SUV's?"

Fred shrugged his shoulders, "I don't know why he insists on me driving, but he drives the other because he thinks of it as his baby."

"Well, I always figured it had something to do with his ego."

Fred chuckled, "Yeah, he thinks women are going to fall at his feet." Fred turned into the lot and eased the vehicle into a slot near the door. He figured she knew how Spencer felt as he added, "Especially you."

She screwed her face up and stuck a finger in her mouth making a gagging noise. "No way. No way in hell would I ever throw myself at him."

Fred chuckled, "Don't worry about it." He pat her on the hand thinking of her as a younger sister. "My wife says that maybe one day he'll grow up."

Jasmine opened the door and turned to Fred, "I sort of doubt that." She climbed out of the vehicle and walked into the store, grabbed a cart. She pushed it up and down the aisles and grabbed foodstuff she knew the guys liked to snack on. She grabbed a jar of peanut butter and a box of crackers for herself. As she turned another corner to look at the meat section, she saw the deputy again and didn't think nothing of it. She stopped in front of the ground beef. Looking at the packages of the meat. Someone invaded her space.

She turned and gazed into his gunmetal gray eyes, and he smiled at her, but the smile didn't reach his eyes. They were cold and calculated as if he were sizing her up, or if she were a slab of meat set on the table for eating. He ran a finger over her hand and then he strode off without saying a word.

The hair on her arms stood up as chills ran down them. She rubbed her hands her arms. She looked all around her but didn't see him. Her heartbeat raced and her stomach twisted into knots. Skip the meat, she grabbed some lunch meat and bread and headed quickly to the cash register to pay for the groceries.

She continued to look around her as the cashier gazed at her, "Not from around here?" she asked trying to make conversation.

Jasmine tried to calm her nerves "No, I'm not." She pulled out the credit card and swiped it as the cashier began to bag up her purchases.

She grabbed the bags and carried them out to the SUV and put them behind her seat. Bella's attention was caught by the rattling plastic. "No nosing around there Bella." The dog looked up at her as Jasmine reached in and rubbed the dog's head. Bella huffed out a gust of breath like a sigh as her nose continued to work at the smells from the grocery bags.

Jasmine looked around one more time and didn't see the deputy anywhere. The man gave her the creeps and the vibes he gave off were pure evil. She climbed into the vehicle and sat in the seat next to Fred.

"Ready to go?"

"Yeah, but I want to stop at the fruit market on the way back. I think I want some apples and check out some of the other fruit they have."

"Sounds like a winner to me," he turned the engine over and backed out of the slot. "We have to pick up Devin on the way back," he stated as he drove down to Jackson hung a left and then pulled into the city hall parking lot.

Devin hopped into the SUV and looked down at the bags on the floor and started to poke through the bags, "Looks like someone's been busy."

"Yeah," Jasmine frowned. "We'll part it all out when we get to the motel. We're going to stop at the fruit market."

Fred pulled out of the parking lot, turned right followed by a left and turning into the lot in front of the fruit market. The rain had stopped, and the sun was trying to peek through the clouds. Jasmine took off her poncho and hopped out of the SUV and looked at the sign on the sign of door confirming they took credit cards.

Stepping inside fluorescent lights hung from the ceiling, and several ceiling fans whirred. The sweet smell of fresh and overripe fruit caught her attention. She picked up a handheld basket and wandered around looking at the fruit in the bins. She picked out a few apples, thumped a cantaloupe on its rough outer shell, it sounded ripe to her, and she placed it in the basket. She glanced at the bananas and stepped around another bin and came face to face with the deputy.

Her eyes grew as he smiled again at her. Her heart raced as the saliva in her mouth dried up as it turned into a dustbowl. She tried to swallow but found it difficult.

He moved up beside her and rubbed a hand up over her arm. "I bet you taste as sweet as you look," he said and purposefully bumped into her to grab her left breast. "I'll be seeing you, soon," he whispered into her ear. His tone was hard but with an edge to it.

Jasmine's knees shook as she took several deep breaths trying to steady her nerves as she looked around her. She almost yelled out loud when she heard Everit's voice in her mind. "I'm coming as soon as I can." Even through his words, she could feel his anger.

Her voice came out as soft as a whisper, "No, you shouldn't. I can take care of myself." She did her best to convince him.

Everit's response was terse, maybe even a bit angry, "I'll be paying better attention to what's going on around you."

She stomped her foot but moved around another bin so no one would think she was crazy for talking to herself. "Look, it's 2016, and women are able to protect themselves better now. Heck, we can even join the military now and fight on the front lines."

Jasmine imagined that he was sitting on his rock in the cave, but was he angry at her.

She shook her head. She didn't think so. She thought maybe he was angry at himself. "I'll still check up on you."

Everit picked up a rock and threw it. Why was she so stubborn about this? Desperate for a way to get out he glanced down at his Kentucky Long Rifle and the powder horn. Think, he told himself. He had to get out of this place that was his prison. Would it work, he wondered. There was still a lot of rock to move, but he didn't think he could move it all, and he had to be honest with himself he could make the situation worse.

All right, he wouldn't try the black powder just yet. He'd continue to work on moving the rock with both his hands, but now he had two reasons, and both reasons had to do with Jasmine.

Chapter 6

As they parked in the motel's lot, Jasmine hopped out of the SUV. She and Devin sorted through the bags, and she passed two of them over to Fred. "One of those is for Roland. I bought a cantaloupe at the fruit market if either of you wants some later."

"Sounds good," he said as he climbed up the stairs.

Devin held a package of lunchmeat in his hand, "So what do we do with this?"

"Spencer says he brought a mini-fridge with him, so it's in his room."

"He thinks of everything," Devin muttered.

She handed Devin the credit card. "Give this to Spencer." Then she passed Devin a bag for himself, then Spencer's bag, and finally a third bag that held the lunchmeat. "I'll let you deal with him and the lunchmeat," she said.

Devin chuckled, "Sending me into the lion's den?"

"Better you than me," she smirked as she grabbed her now damp poncho, Bella's leash, and her grocery bag. She found it a little funny that if she hadn't pushed for the food, they'd still be living on fast food. She chuckled to herself about how men needed someone to mother them. She pulled out the key card and walked over to her room and slid it into the slot.

She led Bella into the room. Locked the door behind her, took the leash off, put the bag on the table, then put some food in Bella's bowl.

Bella stuck her nose into the bowl. Her jaws crunching the food as easily as she could snap a man's arm.

Jasmine glanced around and then smacked herself on the forehead. "I was in such a panic I forgot to get us some water." She made sure she had her keycard to the door. Unlocking her door, she pulled it shut locking Bella inside.

She walked down the sidewalk to the Coke machine. She fed it some money and pulled out a couple of bottles of water. The machine hummed as it's cooling system kicked in. She stopped and glanced around. She had to make sure the deputy wasn't watching her again.

She turned around and nearly collided with Spencer. "I saw you pass my room," he said by way of explanation. "We've got an interesting case this time. It might mean we have to stay there several days."

Sarcasm dripped from her tongue, "Oh goodie. Just what I wanted to hear."

Spencer grabbed her by the arms "Why are you such a bitch?"

"Why are you such a Peeping Tom?" She threw the question back at him as she wrenched one of her arms out of his grip.

Spencer yanked her forward and then lowered his mouth to hers and kissed her.

Jasmine pushed away from him and then swung her free hand and caught him across the face. "Don't you ever do that again!" She yelled as she wrenched her other arm out of his grip and then raced back to her room.

She fumbled with the keycard and tried three times to open the door when she finally got it to slide in the slot. She slammed the door shut and locked it behind her. She heard Everit chuckle in her mind. "Don't you start," she said to herself.

She opened the first bottle of water and poured some in Bella's dish. Her cell phone rang, and she pulled it out of her pocket and glanced down at the display. It was Spencer again. "He can wait," she frowned as her hands trembled. Why did he think she wanted him? She didn't.

She grabbed a knife out of the overnight bag and expertly sliced the fruit in half. She scraped out the seed mess into the garbage can next to the table. She pulled out the bowl she purchased from the fruit market and then sliced it up into slices and put them into the bowl. Her phone rang again. She glanced at the caller ID and then pressed talk.

Jasmine's voice was so cold she could imagine Fred freezing on the other end. "What does his majesty want now?"

"He wants to go over the Foley case."

"If he'd given me some time I would have been there sooner," she said as she hit the disconnect button and shoved the cell phone into her pocket. She picked up the bowl she'd sat on the table, unlocked the door. Bella rushed out with her.

She stepped over to Spencer's room which was just next door and stepped inside. Veiled anger showed in his eyes as he spat out, "Glad you could finally join us."

She frowned and dared him to say something else, "I had things to do, one of which was to get this cantaloupe ready to eat."

He waved a hand through the air as if he were shooing a fly. "Now that everyone is here. Our next case is at the Foley's."

Jasmine rolled her eyes, mouthed back at him, we already know this.

Spencer glared back at her. How long was she going to hold a grudge? He turned to Devin, "What did you find out about the house Devin?"

Fred and Roland helped themselves to a piece of the cantaloupe as they listened to Devin. "There was a house on the property that was built back in the late 1700's that was the home of the town doctor, Daniel Ibson. There are rumors that Ibson was sadistic and liked to torture some of his patients. After Ibson died, no one went near the house believing that the doctor's spirit and those of his patients that died were still in the house. But as the house deteriorated so does people's memories, and the house was razed to the ground to make way for a new housing development in 1972."

Devin picked out a piece of cantaloupe and took a bite practically humming in pleasure as he chewed the piece of fruit.

Spencer turned his laptop around so everyone could see the screen. "This is footage that the other paranormal team got on camera." He cued up the footage. His team stared intently as the table shook as if someone was shaking it. They heard a male voice distinctly say, Help Me.

Spencer stopped the replay, "According to Mayor Westermann, the other paranormal team that the Foley's called in ran away. They believe that the house has a demon, or it was demonic in nature. I don't believe that. We also have footage that the Foley's caught on security cameras they put inside the house. They thought someone was trying to break in."

He pressed play again, and the footage changed to that of a living room with overstuffed chairs, a couch, and several end tables. The picture was in black and white, like a closed-circuit TV. They watched as several balls of light came up seemingly out of the floor and flew around the room.

"This doesn't look like demonic activity to me. It looks more like orbs that suggest something isn't at rest," Spencer followed up.

Jasmine leaned back in her chair, "could be," she just said simply.

Everit whispered into her mind, "I don't like it."

"Be quiet," she whispered, then she coughed into her hand to cover up that she was talking to Everit and not talking to herself. She sighed, Everit needed to give her some space. She tuned in to what was going on around her.

Spencer was still droning on, "The Foley's want to meet us tomorrow, so we'll rest up today. We leave tomorrow at nine a.m."

Jasmine jumped up from her chair and rushed out of the room and raced back to her room.

Everit, amusement evident in his voice asked, "Are you going to spank me?"

"No, but I have to walk Bella," she said. She picked up the leash and Bella jumped up putting her front paws on Jasmine's stomach.

"Who's a good girl," Jasmine said as she rubbed her hands over the dog's neck and smiled. She hooked the leash up to the collar. "Okay now get down." She pushed Bella away with her hip. She opened the door and led her dog through the grass out behind the building.

She hadn't seen the deputy around and hoped he was doing some law enforcement work, and not stalking her. Her nerves were on edge.

Jasmine and Bella came around the corner and entered the room, she turned to lock the door, and the deputy stood with his gun drawn aiming it at her. His gunmetal gray eyes flashed with definite lust. "Lock the dog in the bathroom," he ordered as he motioned with his gun. He took a step forward and locked the door behind him. He pulled out his cuffs from the back of his belt and grinned at her. "We're going to have some fun."

Everit sat on the rock for a minute, that's when he felt Jasmine's fear and panic rise. He concentrated on her and saw the deputy.

He needed power, more than what he had. He opened himself up and reached out using the link with Jasmine and felt the deputy's lust. He yanked his hand back as if he was pulling at something and pulled a surge of energy from the deputy. He caught something else on his periphery. It was larger, it was pure raw anger and a need for revenge. He drew on it too, this would sustain him for much longer than the deputy's energy.

Everit grabbed the powder horn and shoved it as far as it would go into a crevice in the rocks. He moved to the back wall and pulled some of the energy out into a ball. It crackled and sparked in the air as he threw it as hard and fast as possible. It hit the powder horn, and the resulting chain reaction blew the rock that covered the cave mouth flying out in all directions.

He was finally free, but Jasmine needed him, now. He grabbed his Kentucky long rifle and ran out of the cave. He set his focus on Jasmine. He didn't know it, but he was using her as his destination point like a GPS.

Jasmine did as she was told and put Bella into the bathroom, and turned to face the deputy. Her face turned ashen as she seemed to lose the ability to speak. Her heart raced, and her chest hurt.

His voice held venom in it, "Sit on the bed," he ordered.

She couldn't move, it was if her feet were rooted to the floor.

"I said sit on the bed," he reached out and slapped her across the face with the back of his hand, and she fell, stunned.

He reached down and grabbed her, and threw her down on the bed. He pounced and locked one of her wrists with a cuff, pushed it through a slat in the headboard and pulled it through the other side and cuffed her other wrist.

She regained her senses and looked up at the cuffs pulling, trying to get her wrists free. She stopped moving when she felt the bed depress and found him on his knees beside her taking off his gun belt and letting it drop to the floor.

"Isn't this cozy," he said as he ran a hand up under her shirt and rubbed it across her stomach.

Her voice shook as she finally found it, "You don't have to do this," she tried to stay calm, but there was no way in hell she was going to let him violate her.

He grinned again, and nearly let go with a hearty laugh. Instead, it came out as a slight chuckle. "I just love how you big city girls with your big city ideas of right and wrong come into my town. I love teaching you all a lesson you'll never forget."

He swung a leg to straddle her, and she shifted enough to kick out with a leg catching him between the legs.

Jasmine heard him gasp and suck in a breath and reach down to protect his crotch. "That's going to cost you," he growled and hissed. He unbuckled his belt which looked more like one of those thick leather straps used by a barber to sharpen a straight razor. He pulled it out of the belt loops and doubled it. He pulled her shirt up exposing her midsection. He raised his arm and brought it down hard across her midsection.

Jasmine gasped as her eyes watered and she bit her lip to keep from crying out. She was afraid if she did that he'd kill the men she worked with before they could free her.

He brought the belt down on her midsection repeatedly until blood ran over her stomach. Jasmine tried drawing herself up into a ball, he rolled her onto her stomach her shoulders screaming in pain as her arms crossed, and he deliberately yanked her down a notch to increase the agony. She screamed into the pillow as tears wet the material.

Bella, hearing her human barked furiously and slammed her body into the door. She was going berserk trying to find a way out of the bathroom.

    Everit heard Bella going berserk. His senses told him that Jasmine was getting weaker. He saw the motel coming up. His time spent with the Apache did him justice. He'd learned how to travel long distances on hardly any water and food.
    His moccasin covered feet pounded the pavement as he ran into the parking lot. He zeroed in on her motel room. Everit stopped in front of her door and with one well-placed kick wood splintered and the door crashed open as he stood in the doorway glaring at the deputy.

Chapter 7

The deputy looked up. The man who stood in the doorway made an imposing figure with long hair that hung down around his waist, dressed in buckskins and carrying an old-fashioned muzzle-loading rifle. He blinked not believing his eyes. He thought the man was a ghost, but that was the last coherent thought that came to mind as the rifle butt came crashing down into his face.

Everit moved over to the bed, "Jasmine," he whispered as he gently rolled her back over.

Eyes full of tears she blinked several times to try to clear them as she gazed up at his face. "Everit?"

"Yes, I'm here," he heard movement at the doorway and turned to look at both Spencer and Devin staring through the broken door at him. "Don't just stand there, I need to get her free, and someone needs to get her dog out of the bathroom. Someone also needs to take care of this bastard who hurt her," he ordered.

"Look, pal," Spencer began, "I don't know who the hell you are—"

"Shut the hell up," Jasmine cut in before he could start a long-winded diatribe. "Get me out of these handcuffs," she moaned as her shoulder muscles spasmed.

Fred and Roland who appeared behind Spencer shoved the man out of the way. Fred found the keys to the cuffs and unlocked them.

He held the cuffs for a moment and used them to handcuff the deputy. He knew clear heads would prevail here, and he dumped out the stuff from Jasmine's grocery bag.

Devin freed Bella who came out growling and snarling but stopped when she saw Devin. Her tail wagged, but she shoved against his legs trying to get to Jasmine.

Roland ran out to the SUV with the equipment and brought in the digital camera. He pulled out the sim card and replaced it with a fresh one. "I'll take pictures of this mess," he said. "They do this on all the cop shows on TV."

He took pictures of the crime scene and pictures of the resultant beating that Jasmine took. Spencer got on the phone and called the sheriff's office requesting the presence of the sheriff at the motel.

Jasmine's voice shook, "D-Devin, please take Bella for a walk." She couldn't stand being the focus of all the attention. She wanted this to be over. She drew in a shuddering breath as she tried to convince herself it wasn't as bad as it looked.

Devin left the room with Bella in tow as Spencer stared at her and the blood drained out of his face. Finally, he got himself under control. "Who the heck is the nature boy?" he pointed at Everit.

Everit's muscles tensed as he turned ready to take on Spencer, but Jasmine placed a hand on his. "This is my friend, Everit Black.

He's a reenactor. He was in the area, and I'm grateful he was."

He turned back to her and cocked an eyebrow at her.

Her brown eyes pleaded with him to roll with this.

The white car with a yellow stripe down the side pulled into the lot. Sheriff Joshua Delmont stepped out of the car and stomped toward the room. "What the hell's going on here," he said in his usual gruff manner.

"Sheriff, one of your deputies, attacked one of my people," Spencer glared as he puffed himself up.

Delmont shoved into the room, and Roland passed him the sim card from the camera. "I took pictures of the crime scene."

His deputy began to stir on the floor. He glanced at Jasmine, couldn't deny that something happened. "What happened here?"

Jasmine groaned as she fought off another wave of pain. "He's been following me all over town. I ran into him twice today once at the grocery, and the other at the fruit market. He said he'd see me soon. I didn't know he meant," she grabbed Everit's hand and squeezed as her muscles spasmed again.

"I took my dog for a walk and when we returned he was waiting for me in my motel room. I always lock up when I leave so there's no way he could have got in unless he got a spare from the clerk on the desk. He was going to rape me, said he'd done it to other women. I kicked him, and he beat me with his belt."

Fred passed him the bag where he'd placed the man's missing belt. "If you look you'll see there's not only blood but also some skin on the leather."

"Thanks for your help," he glanced back at Jasmine and sorrow struck him. What if he'd attacked his daughter, what would he do? Probably hunt his own man down and shoot him.

Spencer glared back at the sheriff. "Lock him up, he's a predator who won't stop."

The deputy, Lewis James sat up brain foggy from having something smashed in his face. "Don't listen to them, Sheriff. It was just a game we were playing. She agreed to it."

Delmont frowned. "You know, things are starting to fall into place. There were other reports from women who said you did something to them, but they recanted. I guess you intimidated them."

James's gunmetal gray eyes stared at Jasmine. They were full of hatred, as Delmont grabbed the deputy by the arm and hauled him up and out of the room.

"I'll get you a new room," Spencer said. "You can't be expected to stay in a room with a broken door."

"One with two beds would be nice," Jasmine said as Spencer stalked off.

Everit knew each of these men would have put their life on the line to save Jasmine.

"Could someone get me something to clean these wounds off?"

Fred disappeared into the bathroom and returned with a clean wet washcloth and passed it over to Everit who rubbed it gently over the open welts on Jasmine's stomach and repeated his effort on the back. "This may sting a bit," as he pulled the salve out of his pouch and rubbed it into the open wounds.

Roland ran out and returned with bandages that he wound around her midsection and back. Spencer returned and glared at Everit. "Your new room is over in the second building. Room number two." He passed the keycard over to Jasmine.

Devin returned with Bella as Jasmine stood on slightly unsteady feet. "Could someone pack my stuff up and bring it over to the second building to room 2?"

"We'll do it," Roland and Fred spoke at the same time. They grinned at each other.

"Thanks," she tried to take a step away from the bed but then her world shifted, and she found herself scooped off her feet and into Everit's arms.

"You're going to rest. You've been through a traumatic experience, and you need to gain your strength back." He carried her over to the second building, and room two was on the ground floor.

Jasmine passed him the keycard, "slide they card with the white facing out and the black strip facing the door.

He did as she instructed and heard the click of the lock. As soon as he opened the door, Bella ran in. She sniffed everywhere and then turned to them as if giving them her seal of approval.

"Good girl." Jasmine took a quick look around the room and was grateful that for once Spencer had done what she'd asked. The room had two full-sized beds. A TV hung mounted on the wall over a dresser, with a small desk beside it. A roundtable with chairs sat next to a window. There was a small alcove with a small refrigerator, and a small two burner stove sat next to it. A bathroom was on the other side of the room. "This is a nice upgrade from the last one." Though it stank of stale cigarette smoke, it was bigger.

Roland and Fred arrived with her carry-on bag, laptop bag, and the saddlebags. Roland had grabbed his empty grocery bag and stuffed the food she had bought earlier in it. "You're lucky," he grinned at her. "You got a refrigerator and a little mini-stove."

"Well, as long as you don't tell Spencer, you're more than welcome to use it," Jasmine smiled back at him.

"We won't tell him a thing," Roland replied as he stuffed most of the food into the refrigerator. Fred left her other bags on the table to be put away when needed. The pair of ghost hunters left.

Everit placed her on the bed then walked over to the door locking it.

"You might want to close the curtains over there, or Spencer will be there snooping," she told him.

Everit pulled the curtains closed, and the room became considerably darker. "Is there a candle or lantern we can use for light?" he asked.

"No, just flip the switch in the bathroom," Jasmine replied and then yawned. She shifted around trying to find a comfortable place on the bed to lay, and heard the switch flip on, then heard him hurl a few expletives around.

She noticed that his face was smudged with dirt, "You might want to take a shower."

Everit turned and stared at her this new world was strange and confusing.

Jasmine yawned again and rose from the bed and into the bathroom. "I forgot, you're not from this time." She made sure the shower curtain was on the inside of the tub. She went through the steps for him, explaining each with just enough detail to cover how a person takes a shower.

She stepped out of the room, then climbed back onto the bed gingerly trying to protect her abused abdomen and back. Both areas tingled. That magical salve he used must be working on her. She closed her eyes drifting off to sleep as she heard the water run.

Everit liked the feel of the water, not cold like a mountain waterfall and not hot like a pond during the summer. He turned the water off, finally feeling like a human again. He grabbed a towel and quickly toweled off and then did his best to dry his hair which hung down free to his waist.

He pulled on his buckskin trousers, and his moccasins. He held the buckskin shirt. He remembered his Shawnee woman who made these clothes. He would have to find out what happened to her but now Jasmine was his priority, and he had more reasons than just attraction. One day he'd have to teach her, but he hoped he didn't have to now.

He looked up and jumped backward nearly falling. He saw his reflection on the wall. How can this be? How did they manage to put a small mirror on a wall? He pulled out what passed for a comb in the early 1800's and used it on his hair. Everit wondered what they used for money in this day and time.

However, he didn't get further in his thinking when he heard a scream come from the other side of the room. He mentally checked up on Jasmine who was locked in a nightmare. He raced out of the bathroom and was on the bed in an instant pulling her into his arms and holding her close making shushing noises and unpinning her hair from the messy bun. Then he ran his hand through her hair gently and held her close.

Jasmine's hot tears landed on his bare chest, as his voice finally broke through the nightmare. Her eyes opened, and she glanced around through her tear-filled eyes and felt his skin touching her cheek. Her mouth dropped open as she felt and heard the chuckle rumble through his chest.

He leaned back on the bed and continued to hold her. Bella jumped on the bed and whimpered as she put her head on Jasmine's thigh.

She felt protected and safe finally. He rubbed his hand up and down her arm, "Want to talk?" he asked. "I feel you're full of questions."

"Yes," she said as she ran her hand over Bella's soft, warm fur on her head. "Can you tell me how old you are?"

"Hmmm… Well, I can say I was born thirty years before Cortez showed his face in my homeland and our capital of Tenochtitlan. But Cortez was a puppet and not a real leader of men. He left the city, and my mother was arrested. Their allies said she was a witch and they burned her at the stake."

Jasmine sat up and did some mental calculations. "You can't be that old," she said as her eyes grew wide and her body went rigid. "You look like your only thirty at best," she said.

He was afraid of this. "I am, and I'll continue my story. The night before her death, I snuck into where they kept her. She told me to leave and never return. She also said that Montezuma was a fool to believe their lies. She said they were not gods, but men because they bled. So, I stole several of their precious animals and took the gold that was rightfully mine. Then I left and crossed through dangerous lands at night, and crossed a big river. I made it into the mountains, and there I lived with the Apache," he said as looked down into her eyes.

He locked eyes with her, and he opened his mind as images flowed from him to her showing only those he wanted her to see about his past life. Then he stopped not wanting to overwhelm her.

"I'm sorry, about your mother," tears gathered at the back of her brown eyes. She sniffed as she wiped her nose. "I bet you're hungry."

"Well, it has been a long time since I had real food of any kind."

"There's some peanut butter in a jar over there and some crackers on the table. I think there's a knife in there somewhere to spread the peanut butter on the crackers. You can have some if you want."

"Sounds interesting," he said as he unscrewed the lid from the peanut butter and sniffed at the contents. He found a knife and opened the box of crackers. This new world was interesting.

"Oh, and if you look in the refrigerator, there's a bottle of water."

"You want that?" he asked as he looked at the small sized refrigerator, and pulled the door open. As he reached in he was intrigued how a light showed inside and it was cold. "How does this happen?" he asked.

"Oh," she grinned. "It just does," she giggled and couldn't help but imagine him playing with the door and watching the light come on.

Everit carried a tray he found in the alcove and stacked on the bottle of water, crackers, opened jar of peanut butter, and the knife and brought them to Jasmine. He sat down easily on the bed.

Jasmine sat up and dipped the knife into the peanut butter and spread some of it onto a cracker and topped it with another and passed it to him. "Try it, I think you'll like it," as she grabbed another cracker and repeated the process for herself.

Bella sat up and eyed the peanut butter as her nose twitched scenting the air.

"No, you had yours," Jasmine said as Belle gave her those puppy dog eyes. She sighed trying to be a tough pet parent but finally caving. She put a little peanut butter on a cracker and held it for Bella who inhaled it.

Jasmine ate a few peanut butter crackers, drank some water and noticed Everit had only ate the one she'd given him. "Is something wrong? I thought you'd eat like a dozen or more."

"No," he shook his head. "I have to take it slow for now to get myself back in balance. It's been a long time since I had any food. Are you finished?" he asked as he watched her eyelids droop.

"Yeah."

He took the tray, put the lid back on the peanut butter, and slid the tray on the bedside table. He propped a pillow up behind him and gently moved her, so her head lay in his lap, and he ran a hand through her hair as she drifted off into an easier sleep. He opened his senses and caught someone outside trying to see inside the room. He recognized the thought pattern. Spencer was trying to sneak a peek inside. Everit needed to have a talk with the man, but right now Jasmine was at the top of his list priorities.

Water running from the shower woke Everit. It was good to hear the shower running. It meant she was doing better. Hopefully, she'd be able to put aside the attack and get on with her life. He knew sometimes that wasn't the case. His own trauma with the death of his mother and other deaths of friends and loved ones who'd meant a lot to him had set him on this path.

He remembered his past life. Warrior and priest, on the battlefield, providing the rights for the warriors who died. Giving their spirits to the lord and lady of the underworld.

Jasmine stepped out of the shower and toweled off then stood in front of the mirror to examine her body. The welts were gone from the vicious beating she'd suffered at the hands of the deputy. The cuts were almost gone, and she felt better than ever. She didn't know what was in that healing salve Everit carried but it must be something potent.

She wrapped a towel around herself and found Everit eating another peanut butter cracker with Bella sitting by his feet whining. "Well, looks like someone is getting his appetite back."

"Slowly, it's returning. I was actually surprised that I woke up hungry," his eyes scanned Jasmine's face. Visibly he couldn't see any ill effects, but he knew how scars could be carried in the mind. "You look better."

She smiled back at him, "I feel better too." She rummaged around her carryon bag finding some clothes to wear. "We'll have to do something about your wardrobe, but I think you and Devin are about the same size so we can possibly borrow some clothes from him."

He reached into his pouch and pulled out a small ingot of gold, "How much do you think this is worth?"

Jasmine's mouth dropped open then she shut it, "A lot. Where did you get it?"

He smiled at her, "I didn't exactly leave my homeland penniless. The Spanish were after gold, so I took what was mine before I left. The rest is hidden in a safe place."

"Let me get dressed, and then we'll see what we can do about converting it to cash."

She hopped back into the bathroom and threw her clothes on, today was promising to be a hot one after yesterday's rain. Once she walked out of the bathroom, she grabbed her cell phone and started making calls. Finally, she found a contact who knew someone who was interested in buying gold.

She took a picture of the bar and emailed it to him. She wasn't patient about things like this. "I'm going to take Bella for a walk, and I'll talk to Devin about getting you some clothes."

She attached the leash to Bella's collar and led her out of the room to almost run smack into Spencer. She put both of her hands on her hips, "What the hell is your problem?"

"I thought you might need, uhm… you know a little comforting," he said as his eyes roamed everywhere else but her face.

"As you can see, I'm fine," she stormed away from him. Bella even stuck her tail up giving him the doggy version of a middle finger. Spencer looked down at his foot, it felt wet. He shook it and turned to see the dog stick her head up in the air.

She led Bella into the grass behind the building and let her dog do her business. She hated to keep her dog on a leash when in a town or wherever. But leash laws she couldn't get around.

She walked over to the first building and knocked on Devin's door. She was grateful that he had pants on. "I was wondering if you had any spare clothes for Everit to wear. Seems he gets so in tuned with a project he forgets to bring any with him."

Devin chuckled at her explanation. "Sure, let me see what I brought with me," he turned and rummaged through his suitcase. He pulled out a black tank top, black jeans and a black vest along with a pair of boxers. "Sorry I didn't bring any spare shoes with me."

"These will do," Jasmine smiled back at him, "Thanks a bunch. I'll clean these when I do my laundry."

Devin waved as she left his motel room. She really liked these guys. Above all, they treated her like a little sister, and yesterday they stood up for her to Spencer. They left her insides all warm and fuzzy the way they cared.

She walked back to the room she was sharing with Everit. The whole way over to Devin's Spencer followed her. She could only hope that someday the man would grow up and act his age.

She pulled out the keycard and entered the room locking the door behind her. She heard water running in the bathroom. She put the clothes down on the end of the other bed closest to the bathroom, and pulled out her laptop and sat down at the desk looking up gold values and nearly choked when she read the value for one gold ingot. It was around half a million dollars. If he were right about the rest of the gold, then he'd be worth millions if not billions.

Jasmine had to admit that would be a nice draw if she were that shallow, but money didn't mean that much to her. She lived a good life making jewelry and special gems to people who needed her expertise. She'd learned well from her grandfather who'd known a lot of the old ways of the Cherokee.

It was the same for all Native Peoples that she had ever run across, their love and respect for the land was great. However, today they didn't go to war like in the old days to protect their people from invaders.

She glanced at her phone. Spencer wanted to leave at 9 a.m. It was going on eight thirty. She poured some food into Bella's bowl and wondered when the water in the bathroom had stopped.

The door opened cautiously, and Everit stuck his head out. "Any luck on the clothes?"

"Yeah," Jasmine said as she picked up the clothes and handed them to him through the door. "All tags go in the back, and zippers to the front," she said quickly to resist the urge to peek through the door.

Chapter 8

The drive over to the Foley house was quiet. Spencer practically had a meltdown when Jasmine said that Everit was going with them. He'd spewed and spluttered until Fred and Roland took him aside and talked him into it.

Jasmine refused to sit up front with him, and Devin was riding shotgun while she and Everit talked quietly in the back.

Spencer had no idea what they were talking about, but they seemed to be cozy back there, and that grated on the man's nerves. Where had this interloper come from? He just appeared as if from magic the day before.

He knew she had friends outside of their group, but he'd always been under the impression they were female friends. He could try to be friends with her, but would that get her to drop this other man.

Spencer drove the SUV into the driveway of the Foley's house. It was a quaint two-story Colonial of gray brick, white paned windows with matching shutters, a gable marking the attic, black shingled roof, with two white columns that supported the roof of the porch. Three steps led to the matching gray painted front door.

Spencer knocked on the door. A pleasant looking woman pulled the door open and peered out at him. She wore a white top, black slacks, and black sandals. Her mousy brown hair was pulled back into a ponytail. "Can I help you," she asked as the dullness in her eyes was an indicator of the stress she was under.

"Spencer Cross," he said by way of introduction. "We're here to talk to you and your husband and see what we might be able to do to help you."

"Yes, please come in," she waved them into the living room and indicated they should go through the doorway to the right. They recognized the living room from the video that Spencer had shown them yesterday.

Spencer approached the man who sat on the overstuffed paisley printed couch. "Spencer Cross," he said as he stuck his hand out.

"Joshua Foley," the other man took Spencer's hand. "You already met my wife, Abigail. Laurel is at school, and we sent Arlene to stay with my parents for a few days. They'll be picking her up from school if you can't figure out what's going on in this house."

"Can I ask what kind of problems you've been having," Spencer asked as he sat in a chair.

Joshua ran a hand through his sandy blond hair, "We've seen an old man in the house. He keeps on tormenting Abigail and the girls. He constantly tells Abigail to get out of the house, she hears him whisper in her ear. He appeared to Laurel last night and said she was going to die. Arlene has an imaginary friend... well, I think it's one... she says the man tells her he's sorry he has to be mean."

Spencer told them about the history of the house and Doctor Ibson. "I can't say with one hundred percent certainty that this old man you've been seeing is Ibson, but we'll try to find out and try to get him to cross over. Do you mind if we look around?"

"Please," Joshua said.

"We'll split up into teams," Spencer said. He was going to suggest that Jasmine team up with him, but she walked off with Bella and Everit in tow.

Devin strode over to Spencer and jabbed the other man in the ribs, "Looks like your stuck with me." He threw his arm over Spencer's shoulder.

Spencer frowned and knocked Devin's arm off his shoulder.

Devin stuck his hands into his pockets, "Where do you want to start first?"

Spencer nodded to the stairs, "Let's go up to the attic. Most people like heading into the basement." They climbed the stairs to the second floor and found a ladder that led to the attic. Like a petulant child, he demanded that he was to go in first.

Spencer climbed up the ladder, as he reached the top rung he didn't see anything inside but felt a pair of invisible hands grab him and pull him through the opening. He sailed across the room and crashed into the wall. "Oomph," was the only sound that came out of him as he crumpled to the floor in a heap.

Devin hurried up the ladder, "Spencer, hey man are you okay?" He glanced around the attic and saw Spencer in a heap on the other side of the room. He pulled himself up and rushed across the floor and knelt beside the blond-haired man.

Spencer groaned but shivered as intense cold touched his ear. Like the touch of someone's breath as they spoke like that of a lover. "Get out!" His eyes flew open. "Whatever is here isn't happy. It just told me to get out."

Devin glanced around. "I think we should take its advice and get out of Dodge," he reached down and grabbed Spencer's outstretched hand helping the other man off the floor. "You sure you're okay?"

"I'm fine," Spencer said as he shook Devin off and flew down the ladder. Devin shook his head and grinned. He followed his fearless leader down the ladder.

Spencer and Devin found Jasmine, Everit, and Bella on the second floor. They faced the bedroom the girls shared. They look up as stomping sounds like a man wearing heaving boots float down to them from the attic.

Jasmine looks around, "He's angry."

Spencer regained his composure. He didn't want anyone to know that he'd been thrown or that he ran from the attic. "Is it Ibson?"

"I can't say if it's Ibson, something about this feels familiar, but it doesn't." She frowned.

She opened her senses and turned around in the hall. "Something else is here, and it keeps on popping in and out like it's playing cat and mouse games with us."

Bella moves in front of Jasmine taking a defensive posture and starts to growl, followed by barks her fur standing up on her back. Her growls are deep and menacing. Bella's reaction drew Jasmine to the end of the hall. There like black smoke, but it stood in the form of a person. Maybe a woman.

Jasmine opened her mouth but before she could say a word the shadow glides across the floor with a speed that boggles the mind. Extremely cold hands touch her, and she doubled over as if punched. Then she's off her feet and flying backward on the floor to stop in front of Spencer. Pressure is on her chest as if it's sitting on her and two black hands wrap themselves around her throat trying to cut off her air as the pressure on her chest gets heavier.

Jasmine grabs for the hands choking her when Everit begins to chant in a language no one has heard before. He pulls out his own smudge stick and lights it. As it smolders his voice slowly grows louder, more authoritative. He aims the smoke straight at Jasmine.

Spencer mistakes what he's doing and grabs at Everit trying to stop him, but Devin puts himself between Everit and Spencer. "He's doing what Jasmine would do. For once put that damn jealousy of yours away and pay attention." Everit waves the smudge stick around Jasmine, but the spirit is only slightly weakened as the chant continues.

He knows he needs something stronger to break the dark entity's grasp. He put his hand into his pouch and pulled out a bit of white powder, and with a flick of the wrist, it flew out of his hand and into the air toward the dark entity.

A blood-curdling scream comes from the dark entity. There's also the sound of a snap that echoes throughout the house. Everit ends his chant with a war cry. Stubs out the smudge stick, and replaces it back into his pouch.

Bella stops growling and barking as Jasmine lays still for several minutes taking a silent inventory of her body. She sucks in a noisy gulp of air. She groaned as her ribs ache.

Everit reached down to her, and she grabs his hand letting him pull her up to her feet. He turns to Spencer, "This house is now cleansed. The dark entity is gone."

Spencer glares at him, "How can you tell? You don't have any experience doing this!"

Jasmine steps in between Spencer and Everit, "For once get down from that high horse of yours before I personally knock you off it. If Everit hadn't stepped in when he did, I would be dead! That spirit was out to kill me!"

Even though Spencer hadn't seen the spirit, he now saw the after effects. There were hand sized bruises around Jasmine's throat.

Jasmine glared at Spencer then threw her hands up in the air. "What's the use of trying to say anything to you? I'm riding with Fred and Roland on the way back to the motel."

Everit smiled apologetically and followed Jasmine out the door of the house. She paced back and forth by the SUV's. "You know I don't know why I continue to work with him. He's a pigheaded chauvinistic idiot."

"Could be that somewhere deep down he has some respect for you?" Everit suggested.

Jasmine shook her head, "No, he just wants me in his bed. I know what he's up to, and I will not give him that." She sighed, "He thinks he's wearing me down, but all he's doing is pissing me off more."

"I guess that's why he's letting his jealousy get the best of him?" Everit replied as he wrapped an arm around her shoulders.

"Yeah," she said as her cell phone rang in her pocket. She pulled it out, scanned the screen, and quickly hit the talk button. "Talk to me Max," she said as she hoped for good news.

"The buyer said yes. In fact, he's so enthusiastic about this he's sent me the wire transfer. I'll be taking my usual one percent cut but where should I deposit the money?"

"You mean he's already given you the money?" she gasped as she shook her head and closed and opened her eyes quickly.

She could practically hear Max grin over the phone. "Yes, he's given me the money."

"Deposit the money in my account, the seller and I will work things out on this end," she replied.

"He did say that if he has any more, he's interested in buying more gold."

Jasmine's fist pumped the air, "Nice. We'll see what we can do," she replied. She hung up, replaced the phone in her pocket and followed it up with a little victory dance.

"I take it things worked out?"

She smiled up at him, "You bet they did. Now we can get some stuff for you." She knelt in front of Bella. "It's too hot to take you with us where we're going, I hope you understand. I'll leave you with your buddy Roland."

Jasmine turned as the front door opened and Roland and Fred came out followed by Devin as Spencer took a few minutes to reassure the Foley's they were free of the spirit.

He stepped down the steps and went over to the first SUV and stuck his nose up in the air, and climbed into the Escape.

Bella, Jasmine, and Everit climbed into the second SUV along with Fred and Roland. "I need to ask if you can do me a favor Fred, I need to go to the bank but don't tell Spencer. He'll shove that damn credit card on me again. I don't like feeling I owe him anything."

"Sure, we can do that," he said as he turned over the engine.

She hated to tell this little fib, but she needed to. "You know how my car is a clunker? Well, I just got a windfall, and I want to get a new car." She directed her next comment to Roland, "Could you take care of Bella for me for a while. I have a few other things to do after that and I don't want to leave her in a hot car."

"No problem," he glanced back at Bella, "party time."

Bella wagged and barked.

Fred pulled into the bank and Jasmine ran in and swore that the cashier was going to have a fit because she'd taken out fifty thousand dollars out in cash. Jasmine smiled apologetically but ran back out to the SUV and jumped in.

Fred drove over to the car lot, Jasmine and Everit got out, and she waved at the departing SUV. A salesman came over and introduced himself trying to point them to a used junker. If one word could be used to describe the guy, it would be slime.

"We want a new car," she said as she spotted a few identical Ford Escapes to those that Spencer drove and she pointed at them. "We want one of them."

The salesman looked them over. "I don't think either of you can afford one of those," he smiled apologetically.

"You ever heard of never judging a book by its cover?" she replied. "We can afford one, in fact, we'll pay cash. And it must have a moonroof," Jasmine said with a smile plastered on her face.

They entered the dealership which smelled of paint and new leather. She filled out the paperwork making sure Everit's name was in the car along with hers. She called her insurance agent had the insurance changed from her clunker to the new Escape, and within two hours they drove off the lot in their new Ford Escape.

She drove across town and pulled into the little strip mall near Carolina where the Foley's lived. Could she afford her insurance payments now? She groaned. "What the hell did I do?" she slumped forward leaning on the steering wheel.

Everit rubbed her back, "It's fine, we'll collect the rest of the gold later."

"You don't understand, I'm not this type of person. Spend, spend, spend. But you need a haircut, and we should get you some clothes, and maybe we can actually celebrate later."

They climbed out of the car, and she led Everit into the barber shop. One of the guys looked at them only seeing Everit from the back. "We only take men here," he said as he set out his implements for cutting hair.

Jasmine giggled, "I'm just here to wait for him to get his hair cut."

Everit turned and stared at the man. "I just need some length taken off."

The man's eyes stared at Everit. "How much are you talking about?"

Everit put his hand on his shoulder, "Up to here."

The man almost groaned.

"Don't worry, you'll get a tip," Jasmine replied. "I'll be back in a few," she told Everit.

"I saw something in the store next door I want to get."

She walked out of the barbershop leaving Everit in the good hands of the barber. Entering, she went over to the sunglasses that stood on the revolving stand and tried to imagine how Everit would look in a pair. She decided on a pair of aviator type. Then she grabbed a second pair for herself.

She wondered around the store not seeing anything else she really liked, put the glasses on the counter and the cashier rang her up. Jasmine pulled out some money paying for them and exited the store. She walked back to the barber shop and sat down.

She picked up a magazine and thumbed through it. It was one of those for hunters, but all she did was look at the pictures. Time passed slowly as she waited. Finally, the barber declared he was finished. "How much?" she asked.

"Twenty-five," the barber declared.

She pulled out a fifty and handed it to him, "Keep the change."

They stepped out into the blinding sunlight. She pulled out a pair of sunglasses from the bag, then cut the tag off with a pair of nail clippers and handed them to him. She did the same and then showed him how to put them on. "These will help protect your eyes from the sun."

"How do I look," Everit asked.

"You don't want me to answer that," she said as she grinned back at him. Her thought caught him off guard, 'Delicious.'

He smiled back at her not letting his emotions betray him, but he found her the same way.

They drove over to the local department store and pretty much bought out the men's department of everything in his size. They even got him a new pair of shoes, a suitcase on wheels, and the charcoal along with a charcoal grill.

They put their purchases into the SUV. "Okay, we should go get the gold, she said as she leaned back in the driver's seat. You said it was hidden, do you know the location?"

"I hid it in the cave where I was trapped," he replied.

She turned the engine over and drove to the cemetery on Park Drive. She pulled over to the side of the road, and they walked to the cave. She whistled between her teeth. "I don't know what you did, but you sure did make a mess here," as she stared at the pieces of rock all over the place.

"It was necessary," he rubbed a hand over her cheek. "I needed to get to you."

She reached up and grabbed his hand and held it. "Thank you, I'll never forget what you did for me."

Reluctantly he let his hand drop down to his side. He turned and walked to the cave mouth and entered. He looked around making sure no one had come in. He shoved the rock where he sat in their first meeting, and it moved slightly. He pushed harder, and it finally moved more until he uncovered the hole he dug over two hundred years ago and pulled out two large burlap bags.

Jasmine took one, and they carried them back to the vehicle. Jasmine unlocked the SUV and opened the tailgate and made certain the burlap bags were hidden from view in the floorboard compartment.

She closed the tailgate, and they climbed back into the vehicle. They drove over to the butcher shop, and Jasmine bought some steaks, potatoes, carrots, aluminum foil, paper plates, and a twenty-four pack of Coke along with a cooler. As they put the last of their purchases into the Escape, Jasmine smiled at him, "tonight we dine like kings."

"You forget, tonight you're a queen," he replied as he thought back to the prophecy his mother had given him at the age of twenty. It's not the right time to tell her yet. He'd know when the time was right.

She drove over to the motel and parked in front of their room. She got the food she was going to cook and put it in the refrigerator. Then she left him to empty out the rear of the SUV.

Jasmine walked over to the first building and knocked on Roland's door. When it opened she smiled at him, she'd pushed her new shades up on the top of her head. "Was Bella a good girl?"

Roland grinned, "She was good like always."

"You didn't feed her any junk, did you?"

He feigned hurt, "You think I'd feed her junk?"

Jasmine narrowed her eyes at him.

"I just gave her a little cheese, that's all."

"You can live," she said as she grabbed Bella's leash. She led her dog to her motel room and put her into the room, then helped Everit finish unload the car. Bags and boxes and stuff piled on the second bed. He reached up and rubbed a hand on his forehead, "This is new, I think I overdid it today," he said.

"Lay down and rest I'm going to fix dinner," she said then eyed the box of the charcoal grill. How hard could it be to put one together? She shrugged her shoulders grabbed the box and took it outside. In about a half an hour she finally got it put together.

She put it in between the first building and second building on a dry patch of dirt. She grabbed the charcoal and poured some out of the bag, then she added a little lighter fluid on it and then grabbed the long lighter she bought just for this and got the charcoal to burning.

She saw Fred standing on the balcony to his motel room, and she waved at him, and he waved back. She walked back into her motel room and saw Everit sleeping with Bella's head on his stomach. She smiled and pulled out her cell phone and snapped a picture. It was too sweet to pass up.

She went into the alcove and got to work on peeling and chopping, seasoning vegetables and placed them into three medium-sized aluminum foil packages. She walked outside with them and placed them on the grill.

Spencer stormed out of his room slamming the door and jabbing a finger at her. "I didn't think you could be this way," he yelled at her.

Jasmine rolled her eyes, "What's climbed up your ass this time?" she asked as she put her hands on her hips.

He pointed at the car, "Taking advantage of a guy just to get your hands on his money," he replied. "I never thought you'd be that way."

"I'm not!" she yelled back as good as she got. She wouldn't stand for him trying to bully her. No more. He'd crossed that line the last time, and it had hurt her to her core.

Everit sensed trouble with Jasmine. He lay still, and opened his psychic link to her and saw Spencer again in her face. He knew his energy was low, and Spencer needed to lose some of the anger.

Using the link, he used Jasmine as a bridge as his eyes began to glow and he pulled some of the angry energy from Spencer. He started to feel better as his energy was replenished. He severed the connection and then closed his eyes. Spencer would get tired and leave her alone for a while. He rolled over with a smile on his face.

"Certainly, looks that way to me," Spencer continued. He shook his head. What was wrong with him? He wanted to continue this argument, but his energy had just taken a downturn. "We'll continue this later," he said as he walked back to his motel room.

Jasmine stared at him. She shook her head. Her so-called boss seemed to be losing his grip on reality. She walked back to her motel room and stepped inside and walked over to the alcove, pulled open the door to the refrigerator, pulled out the steaks and walked outside to find Roland and Fred near the grill. "What's all this?" Fred asked.

"Well, like I told you earlier I got a windfall," she said as she put the steaks down on the grill. "So, I figured a celebration was in order."

Fred grinned her way, "I take it Spencer thought differently."

"Yeah, he accused me of being a gold digger and that I got it out of Everit," she sighed as she shook her head. "You know I do pretty good with my online business, and I actually opened a small kiosk in the mall that my cousin runs for me."

"Sounds like business is going good," Roland nodded.

"Well, it will be now that I bought the SUV, you know how bad of a clunker I have," she said.

Fred smiled, and Roland just burst out laughing, "You call that thing a clunker. It should have met the mechanical grim reaper two years ago." He said about her old Subaru. He wiped a tear from his eye. Thought about the Subaru again, and chuckled.

Devin hearing the commotion from his own room stepped out and joined the trio. "What's up?"

Fred filled him in on the conversation. Devin lowered his voice, "You don't know the half of it." His eyes slid from the left to the right to make sure no one was listening. "Spencer is literally going nuts." He told them about what happened at the Foley's and how Everit had jumped in to save Jasmine.

Fred's body vibrated as anger shook it. "If you want I'll go knock some sense into him," he said as he finally noticed the light bruising on Jasmine's throat.

She waved him off, "No, I don't want anything else to happen." She flipped the steaks over, then poked some holes in the bags of aluminum foil.

"Damn, that really smells good," Roland said.

She passed the meat fork over to Fred. "Do you mind keeping an eye on this? I should go wake Everit up. I think I wore him out earlier buying him clothes."

"See, now you're definitely going to make some man a good wife the way you take care of us," Devin grinned at her.

She grinned, shook her head, and walked back to her motel room. She entered the room and put her hand on Everit's shoulder gently shaking him. "You should wake up, food is almost done."

His eyes opened, and he had to blink them several times to clear them. He sat up slowly. "Sit down," he patted the bed beside him.

Jasmine sat down, "What do you want?"

"You know how you worried about making that insurance payment earlier. I can help you out." He smiled and saw the worry that was on her face. "Don't worry about him. I'll talk to him later. Contact your friend and see how many more bars this guy will buy."

"If you're okay with it," she bit her bottom lip. "I'll make the call now," she pulled out her cell phone. She made the call and asked Max to call the buyer to see how many more bars he was willing to buy. She hit disconnect, and her leg bounced up and down as she started to bite at her knuckle.

Everit took her hand in his, "Stop worrying. Everything will be okay," he smiled.

Her phone rang, and she listened to what Max said and then she disconnected as all the color drained out of her face. She turned to him. "He's going to take four more. Max said he didn't want to flood the market with gold."

"I don't understand these words you're using, but I think I get the meaning," Everit replied. He watched her stand up and pace as she bit her bottom lip. "Something's bothering you."

"You need papers. I have to get you a birth certificate and other things stating you're a citizen of this country."

"I am a child of the world," he smiled at her.

She redialed Max again, "You haven't deposited that money yet, have you?"

"No," the man on the other end said.

"I need to get a birth certificate, social, a picture ID for a friend of mine. I can't go into details, but he needs a record of being a citizen."

"Gotcha, this will run about fifty thousand. Send me a picture, name, and age, and I'll get the ball rolling on this."

"His name is Everit," she spelled the first name for him, "Black. He's thirty years old. Hang on for the picture." She aimed her cellphone at Everit and snapped his picture and sent it on.

"Got it," he replied, she heard murmuring in the background.

"Katie's there with you?" she asked.

"Of course, she decided she was going to drive your parent's crazy and run off again. She ended up on my doorstep today."

"Thanks, Max, for everything. But please try to keep her out of trouble. Mom and dad are probably out of their minds right now."

"No problem," he replied and cut the connection.

She put a hand to her forehead and mentally groaned. "That sister of mine is going to be the death of me," she said as her cell phone rang.

As she answered, "Is Katie there with you?" her mother asked.

"No, she's not at my apartment," Jasmine mentally groaned. "Mom, I'm not even in town."

"Oh, that's right. Sorry for bothering you. I'll start calling all her friends—"

"Mom," she said as frustration started to set in. "She's not at any of her friends' houses. She's with Max."

"Crap, I wish she wouldn't go see that man. You know he's going to get her into all kinds of trouble."

Jasmine saw a gleam of amusement in Everit's eyes.

Don't laugh, she mouthed at him as she continued to talk to her mother. "Yes mom, I know," she nodded as she agreed with her mother. Which was easier than telling her the truth. Max had kept Katie from getting into a lot of trouble. How Katie and Max met, she had no idea, but deep-down Max was a good guy.

"Mom, I've got to go," she heard knocking at the door. She disconnected the phone and glanced at Everit, "My sister is a pain in the ass. Sounds like she got into it with our parents again and ran off… again."

Everit rose from the bed and opened the door. "Hey, food's done," Roland said. "And Spencer is back out here, Fred is going to have a heart to heart with him after we eat."

"I just hope he doesn't pull anything, I've got enough problems on my hands right now without him adding to it," Jasmine said as she grabbed the paper plates and marched out of the motel room.

Roland glanced to Everit who leaned over and whispered, "Sister."

"You don't have to say no more. We all know about that girl. She was born a hell-raiser," Roland replied as he and Everit followed Jasmine out the door with Bella rushing between them.

Chapter 9

The sun started to sink low in the sky, as they sat around the grill. Roland drove over to the gas station and brought back graham crackers, chocolate, and marshmallows to make some Smores. Jasmine tried to ignore Spencer's stares at Everit who'd managed to eat more than a peanut butter cracker. Devin threw a Frisbee and Bella gave chase.

Roland decided to bring up the subject, "Jasmine, I hear Katie has run off again."

"Mom called me wanted to know if Katie was with me, I had to remind her I'm out of town."

Fred glanced at Spencer seeing him take a little interest in the conversation. "Do you know where she is?"

Jasmine slouched in her chair, "She's over at Max's place… again."

"Are you going to have to go back to St. Louis to take her home?" Roland asked. As he saw the mental calculations going off in Spencer's head.

Jasmine shook her head, "No way, not this time. She's eighteen, I hired her to be my shipping clerk for online orders. She likes it, but she's got to get her priorities in order and stop getting into it with our parents."

Fred grimaced, "Mark's only five, but I dread when he hits his teenage years. I remember how much trouble I got into."

Jasmine leaned forward. "I don't want to continue talking about my wild child sister, I'd rather figure out what we're going to do about this dark entity. I made myself a target when I banished it from Trevor's room."

Roland leaned forward, "Are you trying to suggest we put you out there like bait?"

Jasmine shrugged, "It's a thought."

"No way," Fred stood up. The vein at this temple throbbed as his eyes bulged, and he pulled at his collar, "No way!" he repeated more forceful the second time. "We are not putting you in harm's way. You are our psychic and spiritual guru."

Spencer stood for the first time. "Fred's right, we can't allow you to be bait. You know more about banishing spirits from houses than we do. We'd be lost if anything happened to you."

"That's nice of you to say," she replied with a partial smile on her face, but she was sure he was up to something.

Her phone buzzed in her pocket, she pulled it out checking the text message. **Everything is good to go. All Id's will pass any scrutiny.**

She sent a text back, and then slipped her phone in her pocket. "I'm tired, so I'm going to go to bed. I'll see you in the morning." She stopped before heading back to her motel room. "Would one of you mind dealing with the grill?"

Devin gave her a wide toothy grin, "After everything you put into cooking for us I'll do it," he volunteered.

"Thanks, Devin," she smiled back as she put a hand over her mouth when she yawned. "Come on, Bella." Bella trotted over to Jasmine, and the pair went into the motel room.

Everit stepped over to Spencer. "I think we need to talk. I promised Jasmine."

Spencer glared at the man but followed in his wake as he led the way behind the first building.

"Do you think we should follow them?" Roland asked Fred.

Fred shook his head, "We need to let them work it out."

Everit stopped and looked out over the empty field behind the building. Lights shone off in the distance marking the location of the hospital. Crickets were beginning their nightly chorus along with a few Katydid in the trees in the distance. A few lightning bugs blinked around them. He found it peaceful, and it reminded him of a home he'd never return to.

"Spencer, do you really think that what you're doing is going to charm Jasmine?" he asked as he squatted and plucked a blade of grass from the ground in front of him.

"I don't have a clue what you're talking about," Spencer turned to go back to his room.

"What you don't know is that I've known Jasmine for a very long time," of course he was lying through his teeth, but he felt like he'd known her all his life. She reminded him of his last wife, she was special. She looked out for others, just like Jasmine.

Everit stood to face Spencer, "Look, she's a friend, and I intend to stay with her and help her when I can. If you're a friend too, you should think about doing the same."

"I'll think about it, but why would you buy her a car?"

Everit chuckled, "I didn't buy her a car. She bought it. And when you suggested that she was using me for my money," he laughed this time, "well that was just amusing. You see, she's the one with the money, not me."

"How did she get the money. I know she lives pretty close to the fist."

"A windfall, just like she tried to tell you, but you were too pigheaded and stubborn to listen to her," and annoying he added silently.

"I guess I owe her an apology for jumping to conclusions, but I'll keep my eyes on you. If you do anything that hurts her I can make your life a living hell," Spencer added as he stalked off.

Everit chuckled as he walked off to the motel room. He quietly slipped in from outside, locked the door, and stepped quietly over to the bed. He stripped down to the boxers he was wearing and slipped under the covers next to her.

Jasmine stirred in her sleep, she tossed and thrashed but didn't waken. Bella sat up and growled. Something was at the end of the bed.

Jasmine heard Bella growl but could swear it was a dream, as something reached out and grabbed her by the ankle hard and yanked. She slid down the bed as Bella started barking in a frenzied pace.

Everit sat up, and the room was cold. He looked down at the foot of the bed, the dark entity had its hand wrapped around Jasmine's ankle and was pulling her down toward it.

He snarled at it and then started chanting in his native tongue. As a member of the warrior caste but also being in the priest caste, he learned a few things from the priests. He reached into his pouch and pulled out some of the white powder he kept on hand. He blew it and watched as it floated towards the entity and it turned and ran.

Jasmine's eyes opened, and she looked around her eyes blinking rapidly. "Uhm… What happened?"

Everit pulled her up and held her close to him, "You don't know?"

"I was dreaming the dark entity was trying to pull me out of bed."

Everit held her close, "It was here, and was trying to do just that. Bella woke me up, but you didn't wake up. I can only assume that the dark entity had put you into a deep sleep. What it was going to do I don't know."

"It's female, I know it is, but we have to find out who it is and why is it lashing out at Westilville."

Everit hugged her tight, "I believe you, but you need to rest and conserve your energy."

She put her head on his chest and listened to his heart beating. It was soothing, and before long she was asleep.

Jasmine woke to water running from the bathroom, and to see Max sitting on the chair in front of the small desk, "Good morning," he grinned.

The movement came from the alcove along with the pleasant aroma of fresh coffee. Katie stepped into the room, smiled at Jasmine and passed her a Styrofoam cup. She lunged on the bed. Katie brushed her dark hair out of her eyes, "You've got to tell me, how is he?"

Jasmine shrugged, "I wouldn't know." She took a sip of the coffee.

Katie snorted, "A hottie like that… Give me the deets."

Jasmine rolled her eyes, "No, because nothing like that is going on." She stared and pointed the finger at Katie, "What are you doing here? Mom's worried sick about you!"

Katie stood up and crossed her arms over her chest, her eyes narrowed as she glared at her sister. "Why bring that up. Mom badgers me to death about what I'm doing with my life, and dad still ignores anything I say and always takes mom's side over anything. And now you're taking their side."

Jasmine glared at Katie as her voice rose, "I'm not taking sides! I'm just telling you that mom is worried sick. She called me yesterday and forgot I was out of town."

Max stood up and grabbed Katie by the shoulders, steered her to the chair, adding a little force so she would sit down. He shook a finger at her, "You promised you wouldn't cause any problems."

Jasmine swung her legs over the side of the bed and stood up. Grateful she was wearing her oversized sleep shirt. She strode over to the other bed and grabbed the small bag that held the five ingots inside. "I want to thank you for this, I mean really. Everit has no money," she said as she passed the bag over to Max.

Max was around Jasmine's height. Jasmine knew he was a former army sergeant, but had let his hair grow out some, it was just as dark as Katie's, with some tendrils starting to curl up at his collar. He had some bulging muscles which looked good on him. As good as Everit's looked. Jasmine did a mental head slap and told herself to get her mind out of the gutter.

Max pulled an envelope out of his inside jacket pocket and passed it over to her.
"There's everything you need. I had them make

it a rush job, but the ID and documents will pass any scrutiny."

Jasmine took the envelope, "Thanks a lot, Max." Now she had one less worry to deal with.

The water stopped running inside the bathroom, and 15 minutes later Everit stepped out wearing a tan tank top, dark brown vest, khaki pants, and his new shoes. He smiled, "Good to see your up. Spencer was down here earlier. I told him you were sleeping still. He went to some place called Cracker Barrel, and brought you back some coffee."

Jasmine gasped, and her mouth dropped open, "He didn't try to start anything?"

Everit shook his head, "We talked last night."

Jasmine gasped. She sat the cup of coffee down and pressed her hands to her eyes as a slow smile tugged at her mouth. She lowered her hands, and her knees shook. She took a slow breath in and then blew it out. "Wow, will wonders never cease."

Everit couldn't help the grin that spread across his face. "He said to get ready to leave for the Mayor's office. He wants to leave at nine."

She turned and glanced at the bedside clock, and nearly screamed at the clock. "I'm sorry I've got to hurry. Nice seeing you Max, Katie be a good sister and go home." She smacked the envelope into Everit's chest, "Your papers." Then she ran over to the second bed pulled out some clothes out of the overnight bag, and raced into the bathroom.

As the door slammed behind her, Katie giggled, "I've never seen her move that fast." She eyed Everit who looked at the contents of the envelope and wet her lips with her tongue.

Max grabbed her by the arm, and pulled her out of the chair, "Let's go before you get yourself in more trouble."

Katie pouted as she gazed at Max as she whined, "But I just wanted a second look."

Max yanked her behind him, "No second looks." He opened the door and stepped outside with Katie on his heels.

Roland was standing on the balcony enjoying his cup of coffee. He watched what was going on in the parking lot and doubled over in laughter. He'd have to tell Jasmine about this, later. Katie was trying to dig her heels into the ground while Max was manhandling her into the car. Each time he sort of got her into the car she grabbed onto the door and pulled herself up. Once she'd jumped out of the car, but he raced after her, caught her, threw her over his shoulder and tossed her into the backseat. "You're going home!"

He slid the black lever activating the child lock and slammed it shut. Then he walked around the car to the other side and activated the other child lock on the other door and slammed that door shut.

He turned, waved at Roland, got behind the wheel and drove out of the parking lot. He needed to get back to St. Louis before Katie got out of the car again.

Jasmine jumped into the shower and out in less than ten minutes. She toweled off and dressed quickly in a powder blue halter cut short to show her midriff. Pulled up a pair of jeans, and slipped her feet into her motorcycle boots then brushed her hair quickly, picked up her bag that held her paraphernalia for ghost hunting.

She stepped out of the bathroom and found the wallet she'd bought for Everit. "Okay, this you have to keep on you at all times unless your sleeping. I need your picture ID and your social security card, it has nine numbers on it."

He cocked an eyebrow at her but handed them over to Jasmine. She took the items and stuffed them into a couple of the credit card slots. Then she pulled out some of the money left over from yesterday and put it in the wallet. She handed the billfold over to him, "Put this in your back pocket and if anyone asks you for ID show them the card with your picture on it."

Knocking sounded on the door and Jasmine opened it to find Spencer standing there. He rolled his shoulders and scratched at his arm. "Good your awake." He glanced around the room but avoided making eye contact.

Jasmine tilted her head to the side, "Anything else?" This must be hard for him having to eat some crow.

Spencer shook his head and turned away, "We're leaving for the Mayor's office."

Jasmine turned to grab Bella's leash, but Everit already had her hooked up. She grinned at him, "You know, you are pretty useful to have around."

Everit led Bella out the door, and Jasmine closed the door after them and made sure it was locked. She beeped the doors unlocked, and they climbed into the new Ford Escape. Jasmine turned the engine over, and they followed Spencer and Fred's vehicles over to City Hall.

They parked in the back lot. Spencer tried not to glare at Everit, he was trying to get along with the other man. "Jasmine," he glanced around and stuck his hands in his back pockets, "I want to say," he cleared his throat. "I'm sorry."

Jasmine searched his face to see if he was truly sorry or just playing another of his games. "I'll accept your apology."

Spencer bobbed his head once and then took off to lead the way to the mayor's office.

Jasmine's face screwed up as if she caught a whiff of something foul. "He'll never change, he always got to be first in line."

Chapter 10

The group entered City Hall, and the clerk didn't even bother to look up just pointed in the direction of the Mayor's Office.

Spencer led the way and they all trouped in, the only difference was the Sheriff stood next to the Mayor's desk. The Mayor rose from his desk and stepped around to face them a huge smile lit his jowly face, "Very nice job, Mr. Cross. The Foley's are ecstatic. But they were wanted to express their concern over Miss Stone. They said something attacked her."

Spencer nodded but his eyes connected with the Sheriff's and he didn't like the look of them. "Yes, but thanks to Mr. Black's quick-thinking Miss Stone came through fine."

The mayor nodded and rubbed his chin as if he were troubled by something. "I hate to bring this up, but I understand you went through another horrific experience Miss Stone at the hands of Deputy James. I'll let Sheriff Delmont explain." He stepped aside.

The Sheriff held his hat in his hands, and his hands shifted around the brim turning it around. "Ma'am I'm really sorry, both the prosecutor and myself argued that Deputy James needed to be held in jail, but Judge Wortley let him out on bail."

Jasmine folded her hands up into fists, as her breathing grew noisy, angry. She stood but dropped back into the chair as though her legs had turned to rubber. Her eyelids blinked rapidly, and she shook her head as if to clear it. Maybe she heard him wrong, "W-what did you say?"

The sheriff repeated what he said before.

The muscles in Jasmine's face fell slack, and her eyes grew, "Are you freaking kidding me? I hope this is a joke."

Delmont shook head, "I wish it were. Judge Wortley took pity on him."

Jasmine's mouth and lips trembled as she squeezed her eyes shut. She wanted to bolt. She wanted to run, but she had a job to do. She pushed down her inner turmoil. She wasn't going to let Deputy James get to her.

Spencer jumped up so fast his chair tipped and clattered to the floor. "Did you realize that he has a long string of accusations from Florida to here? Jasmine wasn't his first victim."

The mayor wrung his hands, "How did you find this out? The town council vetted him."

"Apparently, they didn't do a great job," Spencer waved his hand in the air dismissing their concern. "I hired a private investigator, and he's found other charges are pending against him in several states."

Mayor Westermann stepped back as if he'd been slapped. His eyes are wide. The rotund man shook his head, "No this can't be right. I passed his name onto Sheriff Delmont after the council approved him." He glanced over to the sheriff. He didn't want a lawsuit. The town would be ruined. "Please," his eyes pleaded with both Jasmine and Spencer, "We can't afford a lawsuit."

Spencer was expecting Jasmine to jump out of her chair and run into his arms. However, that wasn't to be the case.

Jasmine leaned forward in her chair, "Mr. Mayor, I don't know about anyone else here, but I came to do a job, and I'm not prepared to leave until that job is finished." She glanced around at the others hoping they would agree with her and was surprised to find Bella put her paw on her thigh and bark.

Jasmine leaned over and grabbed Bella's head and ruffled the fur behind her dog's ears, "I knew you wouldn't let me down."

A hand clamped down on her shoulder, and she glanced up into Everit's face as he stood beside her. She placed her hand on top of his. "Thank you."

Devin, Fred, Roland all answered yes, then they all looked at Spencer who nodded in agreement.

The mayor released the breath he'd held as he wondered what their answer would be. He pulled a handkerchief out of his pocket and wiped at the perspiration that dotted his forehead and upper lip. "Good, very good," he reached to his desk and picked up another file. "This one is a bit unusual, but we received several complaints from not only the owners but patrons of the War Horse. It's a restaurant, bar, and microbrewery. The owners are Julian and Geneva Assange, and the foreman who runs the microbrewery for them is named Hal Dobbs. They open at 11 am for the lunch crowd and close at midnight. They're waiting to meet you."

Spencer stuck his hand out and shook both the mayor and sheriff's hands. "Thank you. We'll go look at the place and talk to them. I'll have one of my people go look up any history he can find on the War Horse."

Devin nodded, knowing it would be him to do the research.

"When you're finished, give me a call, and I'll come and pick you up."

Devin flashed thumbs up as he stepped out of the office and went to work.

"Let's go look at the War Horse," Spencer led the way out the door. Waves of heat rose in the air, promising extreme heat for the day. Even the birds and squirrels were in hiding to avoid the heat. He kicked at a pebble that sat in the lot and kicked at it. Again, somehow, he'd screwed up again, and Jasmine didn't see him.

Roland stepped up next to Spencer, "Want to talk about your problem?"

Spencer stole a glance toward the new vehicle being driven by Jasmine, "I thought she'd be grateful when I had the private investigator dig into Deputy James's past."

Roland had an ah-ha moment. Now he knew what was going on. "Step into my office," he nudged Spencer over toward Fred. "We have a bit of a problem with our bro."

Fred knew what was going on. "I know."

"I think that Spencer wanted Jasmine to be so grateful she'd jump into his arms. Now he's got this hangdog expression on his face."

Fred smirked at Spencer, "I've tried to you all along that you can't treat her like one of those ho's you pick up in the bars. Hell, you have no idea who or what they've been sleeping with."

Roland let out a high-pitched giggle. Which is what he usually did when he was trying not to laugh. "You can't treat her like one of those low-life's you pick up in the bar. Jasmine isn't like that."

Spencer's eyes shifted from one man to the other, "So how can I win her over."

Fred grabbed his forehead with his hand and rubbed. Then he looked up. "You know what, if I'd treated Shirley the way you treat Jasmine she would have beat me up and left me for dead. I'm telling you. Real women like Jasmine they want to be romanced, they want someone special in their life, not someone who's going to treat them like a piece of property or a one-night stand."

"Really?"

Fred grabbed Spencer by the shoulder and sighed. "Remember when you sent Jasmine and me out to that farmhouse about two weeks ago? When we came back, and Jasmine told you that there was nothing there because the little old lady who lived there was a hoarder you jumped down her throat over it. Well, seems it was then and there that Jasmine decided that you weren't worth the effort."

Muscles tightened in Spencer's shoulders, "What's that supposed to mean?"

Roland shook his head, "Man, you are dense. Fred told me about what happened. Made me think of something Katie once told me. See Jasmine had a boyfriend in high school. He was a lot like you but he was worse, he demeaned her, and he hit her a few times. She finally got smart and broke it off. When you yelled at her, she saw you as the guy from high school. She told Katie she didn't care if you were the last available man on earth, she'd never get with you."

Spencer jabbed an angry finger toward Jasmine's car. "What does he have that I don't have?"

Fred stared at Spencer as if the other man had just asked the stupidest question in the world. He had one word for his friend, "Class."

Roland nodded, "Yeah, you can see he cares for her. She might think it's just friendship, but there's something else there."

Spencer said nothing. For once he lost his composure and drug his hands through his hair several times. What had he done to deserve all this?

He thought back to that day, and for the first time in his mind's eye, he saw the hurt in her eyes. He considered everything she's said since there and those had a lot of cynical sarcasm.

"How can I change her mind?"

Roland sighed and looked at Fred who shrugged his shoulders. "I don't know if you can change."

Roland added, "The only person I know whoever changed was Ebenezer Scrooge, and that was a book."

Spencer's hands went limp as he stared down at his feet. He noted the sour taste in his mouth, and he wanted to run but not to hide. He wanted to be alone, but he couldn't be. They had a job to do. Internally his mind said to hell with her, he could do better. But his heart still ached. "We've got a job to do." His voice sounded harsh to his own ears. He spun on his heel and stomped to the Escape that he drove.

He pulled open the door and climbed inside and slammed the door. He rammed the key into the ignition and turned the engine over. He put the car in reverse and backed out of the lot.

The Escapes pulled into the parking lot of the War Horse. They faced a red brick and mortar building. A sign over the main double door said War Horse with a rearing horse. Off to one side was a huge double door where the coach could be placed inside the stable for the night.

Spencer and the others climbed out of the vehicle, and he checked his watch reading the time as ten thirty a.m. Spencer walked to the main door and tried to push it in. It was locked. He walked back to his vehicle and opened the file and pulled out his cellphone and dialed the number listed on file.

"Hello, is this Julian Assange?"

"No, I'm Hal Dobbs, what can I do for you?"

"Hal, I'm Spencer Cross, and I was called in to check out your paranormal problem. Are the Assange's available?"

"They're both busy with getting everything set up for the lunch crowd, but I'll come and let you in, I know they've been in contact with the mayor, and if you can figure out what's going on here, I know they'll be grateful."

Spencer hung up, and he motioned that they should go back to the door. In moments a man with brown hair, mustache, and blue eyes opened the door. "Spencer Cross?"

Spencer nodded, "and my team."

Hal let them inside the door and then relocked it behind him. "I've let them know you're here and they said to go ahead and start looking around. Seems Mrs. Assange likes watching paranormal shows and she knows you sort of need to do a walk through to get an idea of what's going on. I need to get back to the brewery, it's in the back if you need anything."

Spencer nodded but didn't say anything. His eyes shifted toward the others. "We're down a man so Fred you go with Jasmine and Everit, I'll go with Roland."

Jasmine, Everit, and Fred stepped into the bar area. They saw metal tubes that ran overhead and then down to some of the beer taps behind the bar. Wooden bar stools butted up against a brass rail that ran down the bottom of the bar. The bartender and a young woman probably a waitress were busy checking the long stem glasses that hung from a rack over the bartender's head.

A swirl of cold made its presence known near Jasmine, and she glanced over that way and swore she saw a little girl with brown hair who was maybe about twelve peep out of the wall at her. "I see a girl," Jasmine said as she pointed past a section of tables in the room. "She has bruises on her face," Bella whined but didn't bark. "She's confused and looking for her mother." The girl vanished. "She's gone."

Fred gazed at Jasmine, "Any other impressions?"

"We need the background information on this building. I feel like there's a secret."

Fred didn't like knowing a child died here. It made him think of his own son.

They walked through the lounge, past restrooms, the beer cooler which was located behind the bar but in front of the kitchen. They looked across the hall where the dining room was located with a few customers for the lunch crowd. Jasmine didn't really sense anything there.

The closer they get to the microbrewery she stops. "I feel anger, lots of anger."

"Can you tell who it is?"

"I think it's male." She pressed a finger to her chin. "He's mad." She stopped walking and doubled over. Hands grabbed at her to support her. She grabbed at Fred and Everit's hands. "I feel so sick," she bent over. "I don't want to go back there," her stomach flipped as a wave of nausea hit. She wanted to run, her brain was telling her to run, get out.

"I don't want to go back there," she squeezed their hands. "I can't go any further." She stopped, and her body went rigid, "Help me," but it wasn't her voice that came out of her mouth. It was different. "I'm trying to find my daughter." She turned her head, eyes grew wide, "He's coming." Jasmine slumped and leaned against Everit and shook her head trying to clear it. "I'm okay," she held her head. "I just never experienced anything like that before."

Everit gripped her by her shoulders, not hard but firm, "If a spirit can jump into you while your guard is up that makes you an easy target for possession. Let's get you out of here."

Fred pulled his cellphone out of his pocket and called Spencer relaying everything that just happened. He snapped his cellphone closed. "Spencer says to continue the walkthrough."

Everit shook his head, "No we can't. Jasmine needs rest." He was worried, not because of the threat of possession… Don't think that way, he told himself. He turned her around to face him as he stared, deep into her eyes. "Can you continue?"

Jasmine sagged once as they continued to move forward in the building. "There's death back here." She gazed around the brewing room and looked for something. "I can't find it." Tears collected in her eyes. The mother's anguish rolled over her.

Fred had enough of watching her break down, knowing she was usually calm and level-headed. He could see she was overwhelmed. He pulled his cellphone out of his pocket and flipped the cover open to call Spencer when it buzzed in his hand, "Yo."

Spencer's voice came through the receiver. "Let's go. Devin needs to be picked up, and we're going to come back around closing to conduct a night investigation."

Fred pumped a fist in the air and grinned at the other two. "Thank goodness for small miracles. Devin needs to be picked up."

Chapter 11

As the team met in the parking lot, Fred grabbed Roland by the arm, "Drive Jasmine's SUV back to the motel. She's exhausted, and I don't trust her behind the wheel."

"Sure, you got it."

Roland stepped up to Jasmine and plucked her keys out of her hand.

Jasmine glared at Roland as she tried to grab the keys out of his hand. "What are you doing!"

"Fred told me I should drive you back to the motel."

Jasmine flashed him a tired smile, "You and Fred constantly watch my back," she leaned in and pressed a kiss to Roland's cheek. "Thank you."

She climbed in the back as did Everit and Bella. Jasmine leaned over and leaned her head on his shoulder. The drive to the motel was quiet, peaceful.

Everit knew the time was coming when he'd have to tell Jasmine about herself. He hoped that she would take the news well, but he had to admit when he learned about himself from his mother it didn't sit well with him. He brushed away an errant strand of her hair that had fallen into her face.

Roland pulled into the motel lot and pulled the SUV in front of Jasmine's room. He glanced up into the rearview mirror and saw Spencer and Devin pull in. "Spencer's here."

Jasmine sighed, "No rest yet."

Everit nodded, "You will, once we get this meeting over with."

They climbed out of the SUV and Bella jumped out. Spencer and Devin both walked into Spencer's motel room.

Jasmine rolled her eyes. She knew it would be standing room only. Fred pulled out a chair and motioned for Jasmine to take it. She dropped into the chair with Everit and Fred behind her.

Spencer spared a glance her way. He saw the exhaustion on her face. He took a deep breath. Why should he care? Seemed she'd made her choice. He couldn't stop the dark thoughts that circled around in his head.

He cleared his throat as he shifted his attention to Devin. "What have you got?"

Devin pulled out his laptop. "Well, as was suspected at one time The War Horse was a former stagecoach stop that boasted a bar, several rooms for passengers to spend the night, and a small kitchen. The man who managed the station was named Virgil Bartlet."

He paused long enough to twist the cap of bottled water that Roland passed him. "Bartlet was known to have a temper, but he was also unlucky when it came to the love department. So, he grew a hatred for women." He took a couple of quick swallows of the water.

"In 1850 a stagecoach arrived with a woman named Loretta Bailey and her daughter Sally. They were heading out west to join

Loretta's husband who was in the army. It's rumored that Loretta and Bartlet were acquaintances. Loretta sold the family home and had a small fortune on her person.

"That evening a thunderstorm hit and Loretta and Sally sought shelter at the station. Bartlet tried unsuccessfully to rekindle any type of romance between them, but she shot him down, hard. So, Bartlet being the man he was, saw the daughter as the problem. He lured her out of the room.

"The story goes that he killed the daughter and Loretta caught him in the act, so he had to kill her too. However, their bodies were never found, but he stole a horse and took Loretta's money. After several weeks of searching the law caught up with him. He confessed that he killed them both but refused to ever say where the bodies were buried. They hanged him for his crimes."

Spencer gazed around the room. "Get some sleep, we're going back to conduct a night investigation," he stared pointedly at Jasmine. "We leave tonight at eleven thirty."

Jasmine rose from the chair, and turned but stumbled. Her energy waned, she felt as though she were all used up. Everit scooped her up in his arms, she didn't even struggle or try to fight. Bella paced along beside them as Everit carried her over to the motel room.

He placed her down on the bed then he sat down beside her. He ran a hand over her face and brushed her hair out of the way. In another day or two, he'd have to tell her. Her skin was warm. He placed his hand to her temple and allowed some of his energy to flow into her. Jasmine sighed and fell into a deeper sleep.

Several hours passed and Jasmine woke to feel recharged and ready to go. She glanced around the room, didn't see Everit or Bella around. Maybe he took her for a walk.

She needed a shower to feel decent once again and glanced at the clock on the desk, ten. She had time before they had to go. She gathered some clothes from the carryon bag. She'd have to do laundry after this case was over.

Jasmine stepped into the bathroom, turned on the shower, and then stepped under the water. She liked this one better than the other one. At least what came out of the shower head was warm water, not the lukewarm from the first building.

She stepped out of the shower, toweled off and quickly dressed in a pair of jeans and a T-shirt. Being inside an air-conditioned building was much better than being out in the blazing heat of July.

She stepped out of the bathroom as Everit and Bella came in. "She's been fed, watered, and walked. I think she's ready for tonight."

Jasmine smiled his way, but her stomach decided to betray her. "I need some food."

"We have that covered too. Roland took an SUV over to McDonald's." He cocked his head and stared at her for a moment. "What's McDonald's?"

She hoped Roland knew what to get her. "It's a fast food place. But since they now serve breakfast all day I hope he thinks to get me an Egg McMuffin."

There was a knock at the door. Everit turned and took both the bags that were passed through to him, plus a couple of drinks. They ate in silence as Everit contemplated the food. It was different, but it was good.

Jasmine parked the SUV in line with the other two in a lot of the War Horse. "I'll show you how to work some of the equipment so that Spencer doesn't see you as the enemy."

Everit nodded, he could see sense in this. After all, Spencer saw him as the interloper, but he could only wonder what the other man would do if he knew his secret. Probably run for the hills. Spencer acted fearlessly, yet that was when he was confronting Jasmine. Everit wasn't sure he liked the other man who desperately wanted Jasmine to see him in a different light.

Jasmine hopped out of the SUV and Bella flew out behind her. She walked over to Fred, "Can I get something easy for Everit to use?"

"Sure, what were you thinking?"

"Maybe a K-2 meter."

Fred rummaged around and pulled out an oblong almost rectangular shaped box that was black with different colored bulbs in a fan shape. They were labeled dark green, light green, yellow, orange, and red. He passed it over to her.

She held it so Everit could see. "This is what's called a K-2 meter. It measures the electromagnetic frequency. The theory states that if a spirit is near it will give off an Electromagnetic signature that can be picked up by the K-2 meter. However, if you get a reading that's very high, in the red, that could be electricity running through a wire.

"We have to rule those possibilities out because high readings can signal problems with the environment that are causing the people living or working there to believe they have a haunting when it's really hallucinations."

He rolled the last word around in his head. This new world he was thrust into could be confusing at times. "Hal-Hallucinations?"

Jasmine smiled, "That's when you see things that aren't really there. Like seeing a mirage out in the desert." At his confused gaze, she grinned. "Don't worry about it right now. It might be a little too difficult for me to explain, so you understand."

"I find it all incredibly interesting."

"Well, that's good." She pressed a button on the instrument, and it lit up. "This is the on and off switch." She turned it off and passed it to him. "Now, you try it."

Everit pressed the on the switch and almost dropped the K2 meter when the dark green light blinked on. He glanced up at her and saw approval in her eyes. He pressed the switch again turning it off.

Jasmine saw the extra nine-volt batteries and grabbed a few. "If anything happens I'll have it covered. Sometimes spirits will drain batteries so they can manifest or try to communicate."

Spencer stomped over to them as Fred passed out equipment to the others. He stared at them, his blue eyes were cold, hard, and bloodshot. "Let's get moving." His gaze lingered on Jasmine. His dark thoughts took another turn as he imagined what it would be like to hurt her.

Fred stepped back from the blond-haired main and waved a hand in front of his face, "Whoa, step back, you've been drinking. You smell like a distillery."

"So, what if I have."

Roland stared at Spencer, "Dude, are you sure you can do this?"

Spencer glared at the others and placed his hands on his hips. "I'm sure, now let's get moving. Fred, wherever that spirit jumped into Jasmine earlier today put up a laser grid there. Let's see if we can get any information."

Fred grabbed the equipment cases needed, while Roland grabbed a case of cameras and cable. Devin had the laptop for the DVR which he would be manning from a base they decided would be in the main office.

They headed over to the door, but Jasmine wondered what had got into Spencer. The man never drank on an investigation or even before one. He wanted to stay clear headed.

Julian Assange met them at the door. "If you need anything you can reach my wife or me at home. I'll return in the morning."

Spencer grunted as he and the others trooped into the building. Spencer went with Devin to set up the base. While Jasmine and Everit with Bella tagging along went with Fred and Roland to help set everything up.

Jasmine kept rubbing the back of her neck and shifted from foot to foot as they set up the equipment. Her gaze kept darting around the area of the microbrewery where they'd encountered the mother's spirit earlier in the day. She wasn't ready to go through round two.

She glanced over her shoulder toward the fermenting copper vessels. She kept her mental barrier up but couldn't help feeling like someone was watching her. She stood up and rubbed at her arms trying to calm herself down. She didn't want to influence Bella, who now stood alert but not in fight mode.

Fred and Roland went to other hot spots in the building and set up cameras. While Jasmine and Everit went back to base. As they entered the office, Spencer handed her a walkie-talkie. "Stay in contact," he said as he walked out of the room.

Jasmine turned it on then looked over at Devin who shrugged his shoulders at her. "I don't know what's up with him. But I'll keep an eye on him from the base."

"Thanks, Devin. Is there anything else his highness wants me to do?"

Devin passed her the spirit box, which was no bigger than a hand-held transistor radio with an external microphone and small antenna. "He wants you to use it and see if you pick up on anything to go along with what happened to you earlier today. He said to start in the bar area where you saw the little girl."

Jasmine rolled her eyes, "And what will he be doing?"

Devin again shrugged his shoulders, "No idea. He didn't share that with me."

Jasmine sighed and stormed out as Everit and Bella followed along. As she neared the bar, she heard a crash followed by a second one. They raced into the bar to see a third glass fly off and hit Spencer on the side of the head. She ran over to him, "Are you okay."

He turned and growled at her, "I'm fine. You didn't say anything about flying glasses."

"Because of nothing like that happened while we were here earlier."

He growled again, "Whatever," he turned and stalked away.

She glanced at Everit. He didn't say nothing, but he didn't like Spencer's behavior at all.

She turned the spirit box on. "I guess it's time to get started." She walked into the center of the bar, "Is there anyone here who'd like to talk to me?"

Jasmine looked around nothing seemed to be in the bar when a terrified scream came through the spirit box. Jasmine's body twitched as she jumped catching her off guard. "Is anyone there?"

There was no response again. The light green light next to the dark green light came on the K2 meter that Everit held. Then it flipped back to dark green again.

Jasmine glanced over at him, "Whatever was here looks like it moved somewhere else."

Devin watching the DVR didn't hear the door open to the office, but the room temperature dropped. He looked around and saw a swirl of smoke by the door as a person began to form in front of him. It coalesced into the image of Virgil Bartlet.

Devin jumped up out of his chair and grabbed for the walkie-talkie. Cold swirled around in the room as the man's mouth opened and he growled at Devin. The voice was menacing as it came from the man, "Get out... leave this place. This place is mine!"

Devin blinked, and the man was gone. He turned his walkie-talkie and using his fingers he pressed the talk key, "Base to Spencer," he released the key, but nothing came back. He tried a second time to raise Spencer but still no response.

Jasmine heard Devin's call over the walkie-talkie. She brought the one she carried up, "What's going on?"

"Virgil Bartlet just paid me a visit, and he is not happy we're here."

Jasmine knew what he had to do. "Get the small smudge stick I left with you and burn it then let it smolder in an ashtray or on a saucer or something. That should keep him from returning."

Spencer walked into the lounge and saw a black mass as it hovered in a corner. He stared at it in fascination as it started to lower and move towards him. It hovered around Spencer and then it was gone. Spencer turned to the door but saw his reflection in the mirror. He grinned wider than usual, and his blue eyes were now completely black.

Spencer came over the walkie-talkie. "Devin, I need you to check out the beer cooler. Thought I heard something around there."

Fred hearing the transmission brought his walkie-talkie up toward his face, "I can go check it out." The response he got he wasn't expecting.

"I told Devin to do it!"

Fred glanced over at Roland and Roland gazed back. Roland spoke what the two were thinking. "He's lost his mind."

Fred reluctantly agreed. "This business with Jasmine has driven him over the edge. I think he needs an intervention."

"He needs something."

The two men glanced at them and saw Jasmine, Everit, and Bella in the doorway. "This is the first time he's acted totally unprofessional," Jasmine added as the trio joined the other two in the microbrewery.

Devin stepped into the beer cooler. The room was cold like a giant refrigerator, with a light coating of frost on the door from where it was opened and closed several times letting in some warmer air. Boxes of beer were stacked on top of each other by the manufacturer.

He looked around and didn't see anything. Nothing registered on the K2 he'd brought with him. He turned to step out but was stopped by something he couldn't see. The K2 started to go wild, and whatever it was in front of him shoved him back, and the door slammed shut.

Devin rushed to the door and pressed on the handle inside trying to get it open, but it wouldn't budge. "Hey," he yelled into the walkie-talkie. "I'm locked in the beer cooler."

No response came from the two-way communication device. He hoped someone else heard him. Five minutes passed, still no one appeared to open the door. He started to pound on the door, "Hey! I'm in here!"

Fred checked his watch. His eyebrows drew together wrinkling his brow. "Devin hasn't checked in yet. It's been fifteen minutes since we heard anything out of him."

Jasmine checked her own watch. "I'll check on him," and before anyone else can say anything, she walked out with Bella beside her and Everit hurrying in her wake.

Fred glanced around the room. He reached up to his ear as if something touched it, and jerked when he heard the giggle of a little girl. "I don't think we're alone."

Roland glanced over at him, "You mumbling to yourself?"

"I just heard a little girl giggle and felt something touch my ear."

"Maybe Jasmine should have stuck around a little longer."

Fred shook his head, "No if something happens back here tonight I don't want her here. You didn't see what it did to her this morning. She could barely stand and needed both Everit and me to hold her up."

Roland knew how tired she was since he's the one who drove her SUV back to the motel but he didn't know the cause. They continued trying to get something on camera or an EVP, anything.

Jasmine and Everit with Bella in tow walked down the hall past the restrooms and stopped at the beer cooler, she tugged on the door. It didn't want to open. She pulled on the big silver handle a second time, and finally, it gave. Devin flew out the door and hit her both going down in a tangle of limbs.

He shivered as his body tried to adjust to the temperature change. "Didn't you hear me calling?"

Untangling themselves, Everit answered for them. "No, we didn't hear you at all."

Devin's eyes bulged as he stomped around and swung his arms back and forth trying to get some heat going through his body. "Nobody heard me?"

"Nope, we didn't." Jasmine looked over her shoulder, "Has anyone seen Spencer?"

Devin shook his head no. But Jasmine's attention was taken away from the walkie-talkie, she heard a giggle come from the bathroom. She walked over and entered the women's restroom. She heard the giggle again, only this time she saw the little girl again.

The girl with brown hair looked up at her with huge brown eyes, "Help me. Help me find my mother," she pleaded as her eyes filled with tears.

Jasmine shook then her torso pulled forward as if in the grip of a giant claw with her arms hanging slightly behind her. She saw as Virgil lured the girl out of the room. He hit the child in the head, and threw the limp body over his shoulder and carried her out of the building to a cellar.

Pulling the door open he carried her down the steps into the cellar tossing the body onto the dirt floor. He picked up a shovel and smashed it into the little body, hitting the poor child repeatedly. Jasmine cried out, she felt every blow that struck the child named Sally.

Everit's psychic connection with Jasmine went wild. He grabbed Devin by the arm, "Jasmine needs us." He pulled the younger man along as Bella woofed and all three raced to the restrooms. As soon as they walked in, Jasmine dropped in a heap to the floor as she was released by the vision.

Both Everit and Devin raced to her side as she stirred. "I'm okay. She didn't hop into my body, but I felt her pain."

Everit and Devin asked at the same time, "Who's pain?"

"Sally's. She showed me what happened to her. I felt everything." A tear slid down her cheek. She needed to find Sally and put the tormented child's spirit to rest. Jasmine struggled to stand as she pushed at Everit who had an iron grip on her. "You can let me go now, I'm fine!" Her brown eyes narrowed.

"Not just yet, I want to be sure." Everit's hands ran over her arms and legs in the quick expert fashion of someone who'd check others for similar wounds or breaks. He released his hold on her satisfied that she was all right.

Jasmine glanced around. She closed her eyes trying to get a bead on Spencer, but she couldn't zero in on him. Usually, the man was like a beacon or breathing down her neck, but this time she couldn't find him. It's not that she was worried – well maybe she was. This was the guy people contacted for their cases.

She chewed on her bottom lip as she opened her eyes. "We have to find Spencer. What if he happens to run into Virgil's spirit? He can't protect himself."

Everit knew she was worried, "We'll look for him."

Spencer looked around what used to be the stagecoach station. He didn't like anything that he saw. Everything was changed from how he remembered it. He walked into the kitchen looking for some type of suitable weapon.

He'd make short work of these interlopers, "I certainly will, or my name's not Virgil Bartlet." He looked at his reflection and grinned. He was young and handsome, he'd chosen well. The man he inhabited was a fool, and that woman with these other men she'd scream. It would be music to his ears.

Chapter 12

Cautiously Jasmine, Everit, Bella, and Devin checked around everywhere they could possibly think where Spencer might be but found nothing. Devin was the first to give voice to his irritation. "This is getting us nowhere. I'm going back to base and see if I can spot him on any of the cameras."

Jasmine put her hand on his arm. "Be careful Devin, I don't like it here."

Devin smiled back at her, "Don't worry. I'll be okay," he turned and hurried out of the restroom and raced toward the office. He pushed through the office door and saw everything as it was earlier. The smudge stick was almost gone.

He sat down behind the desk and checked the different cameras and saw Spencer strolling down the hall toward the microbrewery. He couldn't see the walkie-talkie that Spencer had made each person take, well everyone but Everit.

He thought he saw something in one of Spencer's hands, but the man moved swiftly. Much faster than Spencer's usual gate. He knew something was wrong and had to warn the others.

He grabbed the walkie-talkie. "Guys, Spencer is heading for the microbrewery, but I don't think it's Spencer."

Fred's voice came over, "What are you talking about?"

Before anything else could be said doors started to slam shut all over the building, and wind from out of nowhere blew up knocking people and equipment over. Fred's voice came over the walkie-talkie again, "He's here!"

Jasmine got to her feet, and Bella barked. She, Bella, and Everit took off at a run towards the back of The War Horse. They reached the door, and it wouldn't move. Devin joined them he was anxiously muttering to himself as he slammed his shoulder into the door. Everit sensing the man's panic joined him.

Bella was barking now, furious, wild barking. Devin and Everit hit the door with their shoulders one more time, and it flew open. Jasmine raced in with Bella on her heels. Bella placed herself in front of Jasmine and growled for everything she was worth as her fur bristled and stood up on end.

Everit and Devin took up places behind her as they both saw Roland lying on one side and bleeding. He wasn't moving. Fred was struggling with Spencer trying to keep the knife from stabbing him anyplace vital, but Fred was losing as the grin on Spencer's face grew.

Everit pulled the vest off and tossed it to the side, then he grabbed the tank top and pulled it off. He didn't want anything on that would hinder his movements. He smacked Devin in the arm getting his attention, "Check on Roland," and he charged uttering a war cry from his throat. One that human ears had not heard in over 2,000 years.

Everit kicked out and caught Spencer in the side and knocked the other man from Fred, who even though exhausted managed to get to his hands and knees and crawl over to Roland and Devin.

Spencer glared up at Everit, his eyes were black. "Get out of him," Everit warned.

Spencer glared at Everit, "No, and when I get done with you I'm gonna have fun with your woman."

Everit shook his head, "You can try, but you won't get through me." Both men circled each other and Spencer lashed out with the butcher knife several times, but each time Everit jumped back a step.

"You'll tire soon, Redman, and then I'll have you."

Jasmine shook her head, the voice coming out of Spencer's mouth wasn't his. "It's Virgil Bartlet."

Everit easily skirted around Spencer, and when he lashed out again with the knife, Everit grabbed his aggressor's wrist and then he dropped while bringing up a foot and placing it into Spencer's abdomen. He used his momentum against Spencer flipping the younger man onto his back.

Air whooshed out of Spencer's lungs. Everit knew he was stunned, he jumped up regaining his feet and pried his fingers off the handle of the butcher knife and tossed it across the room. It clattered as it skittered across the floor.

Jasmine went into action and spread salt around Spencer trapping Virgil's spirit in the ring. Everit stepped over the ring leaving his adversary in the circle. Jasmine's eyes narrowed as she knew she had a fight on her hands. "Why did you kill Sally?"

Spencer laughed as got to his feet and tried to step out of the ring. When he found he couldn't leave his black eyes glared at Jasmine. "You think this will stop me?"

Jasmine glared back at him, "You can't leave the circle until I allow it. Now answer my question. Why did you kill Sally? She was just a child."

Spencer squared his shoulders as he doubled up his fists, hatred oozed out of his pores. "Why did I kill the girl? Why?" His voice rose as fury radiated through his body, "SHE WAS IN MY WAY! That's why."

Jasmine now having an answer pulled out her bundle of sage and lit it. As it began to smolder, she pulled out an eagle feather and a shell from her bag that hung at her side. She started to walk around the room spreading the smoke around. Letting it wash over everything. "I banish all evil from this building." She turned her head to glance over at Spencer. "You are not welcome here."

Spencer stared down at the salt, and the wind began to whip up again as the salt started to blow away. Jasmine hadn't counted on this, but she continued to smudge the room.

Everit stayed where he stood, keeping his eyes on Spencer and the salt. Virgil was trying to free himself to get to Jasmine as she continued to smudge the room to get rid of Virgil's evil presence.

He knew she needed to know why Virgil killed the child so she wouldn't feel any remorse later for banishing him. Everit admired Jasmine and how hard she worked to keep people safe from spirits who hurt the living.

Spencer glared at Everit. "What are you, Redman?"

Everit cocked his head to the side and stared back at the man possessed. "What do you mean?"

Spencer's possessed gaze stared at Everit. "Something about you. You're not from here."

Everit shook his head, "No, this is not the country of my birth, but you will never know."

Jasmine came around as enough salt was moved giving Spencer an opening, he charged. But Everit moved like a cat and pounced on the other man grabbing him around the head and pushing down with all his might shoving Spencer to the ground. Everit leaped forward and stomped the back of Spencer's head with his foot. "Stay put, or I will have to hurt you another way." Everit stared down at Spencer.

He knelt next to the younger man and positioned himself so no one could see what was happening. He concentrated and slowly began to pull energy from Virgil. He needed to weaken the spirit enough so that Jasmine could force him from Spencer.

Spencer grabbed his head, the voice that came from him had the quality of a wounded animal, "Stop! Stop it!"

Jasmine thought it was because of the smudging and prayers and demands for Virgil to leave that was hurting him.

Everit saw the black receding from Spencer's eyes he stopped draining the hatred from Virgil. He stood and took a step back as Jasmine quickly bathed Spencer in the smoke, "Virgil Bartlet, I banish you from Spencer Cross. I banish you from this place. I encourage you to walk into the light." She finished up with a Cherokee prayer.

Everyone in the room heard a loud pop. The temperature in the room began to warm up, and the wind stopped. Spencer looked up his blue eyes back to normal. "What happened?"

Jasmine knelt in front of Spencer, "You were possessed by Virgil Bartlet."

Roland groaned from across the room. Fred stood up, "Roland was knocked out, but he just got a nick from that butcher knife."

Devin got to his feet and stomped over to Spencer, his eyes flashed. "You know, usually I like you, but tonight you were just a plain fool. You know enough to never come onto a job drunk, but tonight you were stinking drunk. You let an evil spirit take control of you, attacked Roland and Fred, tried to kill Everit, threatened Jasmine and," he began to shout as his outrage grew, "Locked me in the frigging beer cooler!"

Spencer cradled his aching head, "I'm sorry, I didn't realize." He groaned. "It feels like I've been kicked in the head."

From her kneeling position, she gazed at Spencer trying to find any permanent damage. "We should probably get your head checked out." She didn't feel like mincing words, "For being an idiot and putting us all in danger."

Spencer glared at her, "What do you mean?"

Jasmine shook her head and ran her hands over her eyes trying to stay calm. She stood up and for the first time noticed Bella was now calm. She felt a swirl of cold around her and then a slight tug. She heard a voice in her ear, "This way."

She glanced around but didn't see anything. "Guys, something wants me to follow it."

All the men got to their feet, two with aching heads and followed Jasmine as she led the way to the Cold Storage room where the finished beer was held before it was bottled or put in kegs.

She opened the door and was led to a wall. She moved behind one of the large cold liquor tanks and gasped at what she saw. There was a door that was probably overlooked. She reached out and grabbed the handle and pushed.

Fred stood behind her, "Be careful Jasmine we don't know what's in there."

Her hand shook, and tears gathered behind her eyelids. "I know what's here." She stepped in and found it was outside the building and took several tentative steps as she couldn't stop the tears that raced down her cheeks.

Jasmine dropped to her hands and knees and started clawing at a mound of earth. Her voice was clogged with choked back sobs, but the anguish was clear, "It's here." Bella came to Jasmine's side and added her front paws to the dirt and dug.

Nearly an hour later of digging through dirt and debris from almost two hundred years Bella's paw scraped against something that sounded like wood. They moved more of the dirt away and found a door that was still in semi-good shape for being as old as it was.

Jasmine found the door handle and pulled the door that slanted into the ground. Dirt fell in from around the door. She pulled out a Maglite flashlight and turned it on. Slowly she descended the steps, moist earth, and musty air met her. She saw a barrel of dried beans over in a corner. It looked almost as if it had the day that Virgil Bartlet had murdered Sally.

The others followed her down the steps. Her hand shook as her tears changed from anguish to grief. Fred stepped up to her and took her dirty hand in his as he took the flashlight from her.

Jasmine sniffed and wiped her nose as she used the backs of her hands to wipe the tears away. She pointed a shaking finger over to a corner in the cellar, "Look over there."

Everit pulled her into his arms, and she rests her head on his chest as her hot tears hit his bare chest. He put his chin on the top of her head and just held her letting her tears fall.

The heat from his body soaked through her clothes helping to warm her. She wrapped her arms around his waist. She trembled not from fear or anger, something else stirred inside her as his scent mingled with the earthy dirt smell that surrounded them.

She listened to her heartbeat as it raced and her skin flushed as she was overcome with a need. The need to feel and touch the man who held her, but not here not now. Now she had a job to do. She pushed herself away from Everit, but she allowed a hand to rub absently down his chest.

Everit released his hold on her as she took a step away and wiped the tears from her eyes. He didn't sigh, but he raised an eyebrow as he gazed at her.

Fred moved over to the corner that she had pointed at and found the skeletal remains of two bodies. One bigger than the other. "She's right, we just found the skeletons of mother and daughter."

Roland cleared his throat, "We should call the sheriff and let him deal with this now that we know the War Horse is clear."

Devin shifted his weight from foot to foot, "I'll call the sheriff, but someone should take Spencer and Roland to get checked out."

Jasmine wiped her eyes one last time, "I'll take them. I have to get out of here."

Everit nodded, "I'll go with them and make certain Spencer is completely spirit free."

Spencer glanced over at Fred as he stood up, his legs trembled, and his ribs ached. "Fred, you're in charge until I get back."

Jasmine allowed Roland to lean on her as she leads the way back up the stairs and into the War Horse. Bella pranced around like she was pleased with herself. Everit followed with Spencer bringing up the rear.

They stepped into the cold room and then walked into the brewery, Jasmine stopped. She saw mother and daughter hand in hand. Sally waved, and they both turned and walked into a bright light that closed behind them, and Jasmine knew it was over.

Everit placed a hand on Jasmine's shoulder and squeezed the pressure light to let her know he was there, and he saw it too. "They're at peace now." He stepped over to where he had thrown his shirt and vest and quickly pulled the discarded items of clothing back on.

Jasmine wiped an errant tear away, "I'm glad."

They walked back through the different areas of the War Horse. Roland glanced around. "Now that this place is ghost free, it might be nice to come back and check it out as a paying customer."

Jasmine agreed silently, but she was sure she wouldn't enjoy the visit. Even though the atmosphere was light, a heaviness sat on her heart. She knew it was from the waste of the deaths of a woman and her daughter, and of the anguish of a husband who went to his grave never knowing what happened to them.

To say that it hurt was an understatement. It was one of those things that at times Jasmine wished she didn't have feelings to feel for the dead and the living. But this was the world she lived in. They walked up to the front door.

Spencer moved forward and unlocked the door. As they stepped out red and blue lights flashed in the night. They didn't hear the siren, but the Sheriff's car pulled into the lot. Sheriff Joshua Delmont climbed out of his car. "What's this nonsense about bodies found in the War Horse."

Spencer stepped up, "Not in the War Horse itself but in a cellar, that is located on the property." He wobbled for a minute as he tried to steady himself.

Sheriff Delmont narrowed his eyes at Spencer, "You been drinking?"

Spencer didn't need to lie to the man, "Yes, it seems I gained an attachment earlier in the day, and it influenced me to do some things that I never would have done. One of them was to drink before an investigation. I never do that. I like to keep a clear head."

Jasmine wanted to get away from this location. She glared over at Spencer and didn't feel like forgiving him for leaving himself open to be possessed. She pulled out her keys and hit the button to unlock the doors. "Come on drunken master…" she walked over to the car and let Bella into the vehicle first then helped Roland up into the car.

Sheriff Delmont shook his head and let out a chuckle. He'd go see what was going on for himself before making the call for the hearse from the funeral home to pick up the skeletal remains.

Chapter 13

Jasmine turned the Escape into the hospital's parking lot. It wasn't a big huge modern building like the ones in St. Louis. It had two stories above ground and probably had a morgue down in the basement. They walked up to a desk with an elderly woman sitting behind the desk. She looked up at them, "I'm sorry but visiting hours are over."

Jasmine closed her eyes to fight back the building frustration and the fatigue and opened them again. "We're not here to see anyone. These two," she pointed to Roland and Spencer, "need to see a doctor. They were in an accident." She didn't want to tell the woman they were ghost hunters.

The woman nodded, "We've only got one doctor tonight, we'll have two in the morning if you want to come back."

Everit plastered a smile on his face. "They might have some serious injuries." He added drawing the woman's attention away from Jasmine.

The woman pulled out a couple of clipboards with medical forms attached and a couple of pens. "Go sit down over there, and the doctor will get to you as soon as he can."

Jasmine glanced around. "While you do that, I'm going to walk Bella." She strode out of the hospital. She opened the Escapes passenger door, and Bella jumped out. "Come on girl let's get your business done. Once I know they're busy with the doctor we'll head back to the motel. I need some sleep."

Bella woofed as Jasmine closed the door to the SUV. She rubbed her hands across her arms as she and Bella walked around the hospital. Her brown eyes darted around. The deputy was still out there. She looked over her shoulder several times. She couldn't help it, but it was like being watched. She shook her head and tried to think positively. Deputy James was probably far away by now looking for another job in another state to prey on more women.

The only thing she heard now was her own heartbeat racing mixed with crickets singing. She strained to hear any noise that would alert her to danger. A hand touched her shoulder, she jumped and screamed as she spun around to face Everit. Bella glanced up from her roaming around in the grass to find her perfect spot. She woofed and went back to her business.

Jasmine touched a hand to her heart as her breath whooshed out of her lungs, "You scared me."

Everit pulled her into his arms, "I'm sorry."

Jasmine settled into his embrace, now she felt safe. She closed her eyes and listened to the rhythmic beating of his heart as hers slowed to match his beat for beat. "I could stay this way forever."

Everit smiled. He brushed her hair out of her face and stared deeply into her brown eyes. He pressed a kiss to her forehead. He knew how she felt about him now, but it wasn't time yet. It would be soon, and then she would either love him, fear him, or hate him. He didn't want to lose her, but that was the way the world worked sometimes. He'd gone down this road before once with a Comanche woman, but she resisted, and she threw herself into a fire.

He'd have to choose his words carefully, but that wasn't for today. He glanced around, and his skin crawled. They were being watched. "We should head back to the car."

Jasmine glanced over, and Bella was finished, and she loped over to the pair and jumped up on her hind legs while her front legs rested with one paw on Everit and the other paw on Jasmine. A laugh bubbled up from her chest, "I think she wants to join us."

Everit threw his head back and laughed. He ran a hand over Bella's head. "Girl there's just some things you can't be a part of." He chuckled again as Bella snuffled at him as if she were saying, 'no way human.' He pat her head. "We should go."

Jasmine looked back toward the small hospital building. "Back inside?"

Everit shook his head, his dark black hair swung with the movement of his shoulders. "Back to the motel. Roland said he'll stick around here. The said he's going to keep Spencer tonight for observation."

Just the mention of the blond man's name set Jasmine's nerves on edge as she ground her teeth together. "He's got to learn, I don't like him in any girlfriend capacity. I can look over his holier than thou ego because he gets us some interesting cases, but this last one—"

Everit put a hand over her mouth and listened closely to the night sounds. The crickets had stopped chirping. "Let's go," he grabbed her by the hand and tugged her behind him to the SUV. "Get in."

Jasmine fished her keys out of her pocket and opened the driver's door. Everit held open the passenger door as Bella leaped in and jumped into the back he climbed in after her.

Jasmine stuck the key into the ignition and turned the engine over. She turned on the lights but didn't see anything. She put the vehicle into reverse and backed out of the slot and then shifted it into drive.

Everit glanced around again. He saw a figure standing off to the side of the building. The deputy who was hunting Jasmine. This made it a little more problematic. He knew what the deputy wanted, but Everit would not give her up. He sort of wished he was back in his own time. He knew how to deal with a man like that, but this new time was confusing.

He was learning, but it was difficult for a man who was in his element in 1811 but waking into this new world of 2016. All these new rules, new things he needed to know. One day it would become second nature to him, but until that time he would look to Jasmine to continue to teach him these new ways. While he would teach her the old ways to add to her knowledge to combat dark spirits.

      He inhaled through his nose and let the air out through his mouth as he pushed his shoulders back. He dismissed his negative thoughts. He yawned the events from earlier were catching up to him. What they both needed was sleep.

Chapter 14

Jasmine woke to her cell phone ringing. She didn't remember driving to the motel. But she must have since the clock stared at her with the time shining back at her of seven am. She reached out and grabbed the phone and hit the answer button not looking to see who was calling.

Her voice was thick, and her tongue was trying to stick to the roof of her mouth, "Hello," she managed to say through her brain was sleep-fogged.

Fred's voice came through the phone, "We just got back. We stopped by the hospital. They're keeping Spencer for another day, but we've got Roland with us. Just thought you'd like to know."

Jasmine absently nodded but stopped knowing Fred couldn't see her through the device. Her body was too tired, forcing Bartlet out of Spencer had taken more out of her than she'd thought. "Thanks, Fred," she sighed into the phone. "I'm really beat."

"Get some rest. I'm certain the mayor will be calling either today or tomorrow. If he calls today, I'll do the meet with him."

Jasmine yawned, "Sorry."

"Don't apologize, just hang up," he chuckled. "Get some sleep." The line disconnected and Jasmine barely got the phone back on the bedside table as her eyes shut.

Jasmine woke and heard men talking. She opened her eyes as the door opened and Everit walked in. She groaned and threw the blanket over her head. She wanted to go back to sleep. The bed dipped and creaked next to her. Her voice was muffled a bit by the blanket. "No, I don't want to get up."

Everit spoke, his voice masculine yet pleasant to listen to. "You can go back to sleep. I'm going over to Elijah Wilson's house with Fred and Devin. The mayor called and said something is going on in the historical home and he wants us to check it out. We're just doing a walkthrough today, but tomorrow Fred's planning on a full investigation."

Jasmine sat up. Her strawberry blond hair was a tangled mess. "Okay, but you be careful and tell Fred and Devin to be careful. Keep your guard up."

"Don't worry," he leaned over and placed a kiss on her cheek. "We'll be back before you know it."

Jasmine lay back down and pulled the covers up around her shoulders. He frowned, she was getting weaker. He placed his hand up to her temple and focused. He allowed more of his energy to flow into her. After this investigation, he'd have to tell her. He removed his hand and looked down at her one more time before he strode out of the motel room making certain the door was locked behind him.

Her dreams were peppered with images from a different land, a different society. It was all a blur as people wearing clothes of many colors and designs walked down streets, past oddly shaped pyramids. She saw someone in the square she was sure she knew who it was. People pushed past her and rushed to the biggest pyramid in the city. At the top, a man in a cloak wearing a huge headdress lifted a ceremonial knife and plunged it into a sacrifices chest and pulled out the victims still beating heart.

She sat up and held her face in her hands. Why would she dream of that? Was it because Everit came from there? She threw the blanket aside. She had to get up and get moving. Bella needed to be walked and needed to be fed. She swung her feet over the side of the bed and stood up.

Jasmine pulled out the last of her clean clothes. She sighed, either she was going to have to wash clothes today, or she would have to go buy some more. Maybe it would be a good idea to treat the guys to another home-cooked meal. They'd like that, but her thoughts shifted back to Everit again. Officially, they were sleeping together, but they hadn't done anything of a sexual nature.

She couldn't help thinking maybe they should take their relationship to the next level. Her phone buzzed, and she picked it up, a text from Katie. **I'm at your place. Had to get away from parents. They won't back off.**

Jasmine rolled her eyes. All Katie could ever do was complain about their parents always on her case about the men she went out with. But she knew that Katie did love their parents, but Katie was a free spirit, and would always be one.

Wish I could talk. Got things to do.

Bet you do. Tell that hot guy to treat you nice.

Don't wreck my apartment.

Blah, blah, blah. Your apartment is fine. Later, K.

Jasmine set the phone down, hopped in the shower and let the water caress her body as she washed away the exhaustion from the investigation of the night before. She stepped out and toweled off then dressed and decided to let the sun dry her hair as she brushed it out.

Bella was waiting for her as she stepped out of the bathroom, prancing. "I know you want to go do your business." She moved over to the bed and pulled on a pair of socks then stomped her feet down into her boots. Picking up Bella's leash she attached it to her dog's collar and picked up her cellphone and key card.

She unlocked the deadbolt and pulled the door open and then closed it behind her as she led Bella to behind the building. Once Bella was finished they went back to the motel and Jasmine pulled out a phone book, and just her luck she found a laundromat nearby. She put food and water in Bella's bowl. "I'll be back girl. I can't take you with me."

Bella looked up once from her food as if to say okay but be careful. Jasmine put all her clothes and Everit's into the carry-on bag and left the motel. She climbed into the SUV and pulled out of the lot and drove to the laundromat. She loaded the clothes into two washers and bought some quarters and some detergent from the attendant. And got the machines going. She guessed they'd be done in about forty-five minutes.

Jasmine stepped out into the sunlight and walked down the sidewalk to the fruit market. There she bought some fresh fruit and vegetables. She yawned trying to fight off the need for sleep. She couldn't put her finger on it. She'd never experienced this before, but she could sleep for a week.

As she walked back to the laundromat, a wave of dizziness hit her, and she had to lean against a building for support until it subsided. She made it to the laundromat and stepped inside, the heat from the dryers mingled with the cool of the AC dropping the heat to comfortable, but still a few drops of sweat beaded on her forehead.

Jasmine put the bags down from the fruit market on a chair beside her. She walked over to the washing machine and groaned. Time seemed to have slowed to a nauseating crawl as she waited for the rinse cycle to start.

She closed her eyes, and more images flashed behind her eyelids. Different people from different places. A man traveling alone. It tugged at her heart. She didn't want him to be alone no more, and he didn't have to be.

She opened her eyes and sat in a chair and pulled out an orange from the bag, she peeled it and then pulled out a section of the orange popping it into her mouth. The orange was juicy and filled her mouth with its sweet yet tangy flavor. She chewed and then swallowed and ate the rest. She figured something with Vitamin C in it might help to boost her immune system if that's what was her problem.

After finishing the orange and throwing the peel away, she checked the washers which were on their spin cycle. She went to the public restroom and washed off the acidic and tacky feel left on her hands from the orange peel. Returning she found the washers had stopped. She transferred the now clean clothes to a couple of dryers, inserted coins into the machines and got them started. Jasmine took her seat and crossed her arms over her chest and sat there and dozed.

Several times the door opened, and the heat from outside washed over her as people entered to wash their own laundry. She heard the chair creak next to her, and she opened one eye to see Everit sitting next to her. She wanted to know how he knew where to find her, but she knew. It was their psychic connection.

She leaned over and set her head on his shoulder as he put his arm around her. "You found me again."

"Yes, I did," he wanted to say more, but this wasn't the place to do so. "So, what is this place?"

Jasmine explained to him what a laundromat was used for and how once the dryers stopped they'd have clean and dry clothes again.

He looked around the room. "So, this is better than washing the clothes at a stream and beating them on rocks to get them clean."

"You bet it's better. This way my hands don't get all pruny," she smiled.

"Do you want to hear about the house of Elijah Wilson?"

Jasmine sat up, "Yes I do. I need to know what I'm getting into."

Everit leaned back and stuck his legs out crossing his ankles. "It's a huge house. We're going to go back tonight and begin the investigation, but the caretaker said he saw some teens running away last night. He thinks they might have stirred up something, but I'm not sure."

Jasmine's brown eyes blinked, and she sat back thinking about it, all the hauntings they'd been to. "I think I need to talk to the mayor. I think he's holding something back, something that we might have needed to know from the beginning."

Everit turned toward her, "What are you suggesting?"

Jasmine chewed on her bottom lip for a moment. "The number of hauntings in this town for one. I mean usually we get one or two calls for one town, but this is on the scale of huge. It's rare for a town to be this haunted unless we're talking about a place like Savannah, Georgia or even New Orleans down in Louisiana."

She stood up and paced as her mind sorted through the puzzle. She snapped her fingers, she knew what it was. Or at least hoped she knew what it was. "This dark entity from the beginning has shown its face at all these hauntings. I hadn't thought to connect the dots, but now that I am I still need to know what started all this. I think the mayor may have the answer and if he does, well we'll just have to get the information out of him. After we're done here, I need to talk to the others and see what they think."

She heard the distinctive whump of the dryers stopping. "And there we go," she smiled at Everit as she stood up and pulled out clothes and folded them. Everit joined her and stashed the now clean clothes into the carryon bag. About a half an hour later they were finished, and Everit pulled the strap of the carry-on bag over his shoulder and picked up the bag of fruit and vegetables, and they stepped out into the heat.

Jasmine pulled into the motel lot and hurried over to Fred's room. She beat on his door, and when he opened the door, she told him her theory. "I think you're onto something and we'll have to take it up with the mayor."

He grabbed his cellphone and called the mayor's office. He paced back and forth across the carpet when he talked. He hung up with a gleam in his eye as he turned to her. "You're definitely onto something. He was totally evasive with me about it, but he'll meet us at the house tonight."

She glanced over at Fred, "Do you have the key to Spencer's room. It would help if we could look at a map. I have this feeling everything started with Trevor." She didn't like giving voice to her hunch, but there it was out in the open but worse she didn't like having children involved.

Fred passed the key card over to her. She raced down the steps to Spencer's room and unlocked it. Stepping inside she saw the mess of beer bottles from yesterday their investigation at the War Horse. The room stank of stale beer. She found his briefcase and opened it and inside found the map. Grabbing a pen, she started from Trevor's, and drew lines on the map and saw it was turning back towards the forest and Trevor's family.

Jasmine threw the pen down and rolled the map up, pulled the door to behind her and flew back up the stairs. Desperation giving her a burst of energy, as she passed the key back to Fred. She unrolled the map and showed him the path that was on the paper. "You can see where it's heading back to."

Fred rubbed at his forehead, concern shadowed his eyes as he glanced up at her. "If this is correct and it's heading back to where it started from we've got to warn Trevor's family and get them moved somewhere else."

Jasmine nodded as cold fear reached into her chest and squeezed her heart so much it hurt. She liked Trevor, he was a cute kid. "We can tell the mayor to have them taken into protective custody or something."

Fred nodded. "We'll do it, now get some rest if you can. You still look beat. We told the caretaker we'd be there at nine tonight."

Chapter 15

Two shiny black SUV's drove down the gravel drive toward Elijah Wilson's home now turned into a museum. The man had founded Westilville, he was the great patriarch of the town, so it made sense for the town to turn it into a tourist attraction.

Red taillights flashed in the night as the vehicles parked next to a black Lincoln Town Car. As the ghost hunters climbed out of their vehicles, Fred carried the map with him. He nodded toward the mayor and spread the map out on top of the hood of the Escape. "What's going on in this town, sir?" Fred gave him respect out of his job description, but he'd lost respect for the man earlier that afternoon.

Mayor Westermann cleared his throat. "I wasn't sure if I believed the old legend or not. So, I went back to the hall of records and found an old book dated back to the early days of Westilville. Before the town grew past a small frontier town, there was an old shack off in the woods home to an old lady. People said she was crazy but according to legend she died in the shack and her well dried up."

He walked back to the car and returned with a water bottle. He unscrewed the cap and took a swallow of the liquid. "One day about 1800 a group of men rode into town. They were looking for people to help them find a killer, they believed she had gone into the forest."

Everit listened to the tale with interest. It was about the same time he'd lived with the Shawnee. He must have been out trapping at the time the men had ridden through looking for this killer.

Mayor Westermann continued his tale, "According to the story, the killer was a woman, but they didn't go into detail about her. A few of the men joined the group, but they lost her somewhere around the old woman's shack. They did search the area but the shack falling apart."

Jasmine stepped up, "But how does this shack in the forest connect with the hauntings?"

The mayor shrugged his shoulders, "I don't know."

Fred stared at the mayor. "I'd like to suggest that Trevor's family is moved. If this dark entity that we've been running into is heading back toward Trevor and his family we want to make sure he's out of harm's way."

Mayor Westermann locked eyes on Fred, "I'll do what I can. I'll call Sheriff Delmont and have him move the family. The best possible location would be the motel." He turned to walk away but stopped and craned his head around to add, "You might want to talk to the curator of the museum. He's returning tomorrow from St. Louis. His name is Marcus DuFrain."

Fred turned to the others, "Well, let's get busy." Fred knew everyone, well everyone other than Everit, knew what their jobs were. He'd let Jasmine deal with the mystery man, but he had to admit that Everit was a welcome change to the group, and Jasmine seemed happy.

The team grabbed their equipment and walked toward the house. Their shoes crunching across the gravel. A breeze rustled through the trees, the leaves murmured as if whispering of danger.

They walked past manicured hedges and stepped up on the huge porch. The door opened and was met by the caretaker. "I'm just getting ready to leave for the night," the man passed a key over to Fred. "Just lock up and slide the keys through the slot in the door." He gave them a slight wave and then hurried across the porch and down the steps as if the devil himself were after him.

Roland glanced around, "I don't think I like this. Looks like he's afraid. I have a feeling we're in for a fight tonight."

Jasmine poked him in the side, "Don't tell me you're afraid?"

Roland rubbed at his side and stared down into her eyes. "I'm not afraid of a ghost. We've seen what this dark entity can do…" he paused and rubbed a hand over his arm. "Maybe it's my mind working me up, but I swear I feel like we're being watched."

Devin gave Roland's shoulder a playful shove, "It's just your imagination that's got you all worked up."

Jasmine knew that Roland was telling the truth, she felt it too. She looked down at Bella. Her fur slightly bristled, and her head was perked up. Her ears lifted as if she heard something.

They entered the house the house, and their heels echoed across the waxed hardwood floor. They stepped across the foyer and into the living room with antique furniture dotting the room with a huge fireplace strategically placed for warmth in the fall, winter, and early spring months. Heavy curtains hung around large windows. The floor was, and furniture polish scented the air.

A huge painting hung over the fireplace. A gold nameplate sat upon the frame announcing the man in the picture was Elijah Wilson. In place of the original candles and hurricane, lanterns were now electric lights causing the room to glow.

Fred turned to the others. "We're a man short so Devin you go with Jasmine and Everit. Roland and I will start setting up the equipment."

Devin nodded, "I'll look for a good spot to set up the DVR equipment."

Jasmine, Devin, Everit, and Bella took off wandering around the house, they found the library. As they stepped into the huge that smelled of dust, leather, and ink, Devin found the writing desk. "This will be a perfect area to set up the DVR."

He pulled out his laptop and the DVR and hooked them up, then he pulled out his battery charger and set them to his cell phone to signal when a battery needed charging. He pulled out his walkie-talkie and depressed the button. "DVR is set up in the library. We're good to go here." He released the button.

Fred's voice answered him, "Okay we've two laser grids set up in one of the hotspots and a camera to record it."

Devin hit a few buttons on the laptop and soon an image of the room where the laser grids were in focus on the DVR. Soon the DVR screen was filled with the images. He slid a disk into the DVR to record the information on.

Forty-five minutes passed, and they all heard Fred's voice over the walkie-talkies. "Okay, we're going lights out."

Darkness shrouded the house, and an eerie quiet settled over everything. Jasmine, Bella, Everit, and Devin began to move about the house after their eyes adjusted to the darkness. Jasmine saw an ominous blur out the corner of her eye. "What was that?"

Devin didn't see it, "Nothing. Calm down, you're letting Roland's nerves get to you."

She knew she wasn't seeing things and stepped into a room. A lilac perfume hung heavy in the air. Devin jerked and rubbed at his ear as if someone had touched it. He shrugged it off as nothing.

Jasmine stepped forward, "Hello, is anyone here?"

Silence.

Devin, who was using the spirit box thought he heard something come through it. He listened again, but nothing came over the speaker. "I don't think anything's here. Let's try another room."

They walked into the hallway and took a few steps down to a sitting room, but it was another dead end. Jasmine glanced around, "Let's try upstairs. I'm feeling a definite pull towards the upstairs."

They walked down a hallway toward the stairs when it started growing colder. The K2 meter Everit held started buzzing and the lights blinked. The closer they got to the stairs the colder it got until Jasmine started to see her breath in front of her. Bella started to growl.

Devin was halfway up the stairs when he heard a cackling laugh come through the spirit box. "Something's definitely here." Then he rose into the air and flew down the steps and landed by Jasmine and Everit.

Jasmine saw dark shadow figure on the top of the stairs. Jasmine pulled out her sage and lighter and ran up the stairs. She was going to stop this entity. She wasn't going to allow it to hurt a child.

Everit knelt by Devin who was just stunned, and he looked up to see the dark figure behind Jasmine as she finally got the sage lit. "Jasmine," he called out to her.

Jasmine turned to see what Everit wanted when a heavy, yet intensely cold hand rest on her shoulder. She felt another cold hand on her back, and then a force smacked her hard as it pushed. She tumbled down the stairs and smacked into the wall next to the landing.

Devin started getting his feet up under him and watched as Everit rushed over to her. "No, don't move her. She could have a serious injury."

Jasmine groaned and heard them moving around her. "The dark entity…" she managed to get out as her brain fogged.

Everit placed his hand on her shoulder, "I'll take care of it," he ground from between his teeth. He should have been with her, but the entity tossing Devin had shocked him. Now he would drive it from this house.

He heard Devin talking over the walkie-talkie to Fred, and Fred saying they were done if both Devin and Jasmine were hurt. Everit eyes blazed in fury as he glanced over his shoulder at Devin. "Stay with her."

He climbed the stairs slowly as his eyes scanned for the dark entity. He saw her, the figure standing near the top of the steps. He heard her voice cackle with dark laughter, "Die!"

He gazed at the dark entity as his eyes began to glow drawing her energy within him. He reached into a pocket and pulled out a handful of the white powder he carried. He began to chant. These unknown words held power to a culture that was swallowed by the Spanish Empire.

These were words were for Mictlanteutli and Mictlancihuatl the Lord and his Queen of the Underworld. His eyes glowed as he pulled energy from the dark entity as his voice grew louder.

Fred and Roland raced down the hall to the stairs and knelt with Devin beside Jasmine keeping her in place as Fred examined her for any broken bones. They stopped and looked around trying to find the source of this new sound. They heard native drums beating, but none of them saw the tall warrior who appeared in full regalia as if in answer to Everit's prayers who jabbed a spear at the dark entity.

At the same time, Everit tossed the white powder onto the entity who screamed in rage and pain and then it disappeared. His prayers stopped, the warrior disappeared, and the air felt lighter. He silently thanked the god and goddess of the underworld. She was gone. He ran down the steps, "The entity is gone. How's Jasmine?"

Jasmine glanced up at him, "Scraped, bruised, and weak again."

Everit scooped her up off the floor. Fred glanced around, "I swear that while you were doing whatever you were doing, I heard drums beating."

Everit's head bobbed once. "You did, I was calling upon my ancestors to join me in the battle against the dark entity." Of course, it was a slight lie. How could he tell them that he praying to gods he hadn't prayed to for over two thousand years? He was sure they wouldn't understand. The only one who did was Jasmine, and she was weaker than earlier today. Tomorrow night he would have to tell her.

He carried her outside the SUV that Jasmine had bought for their use. And loaded her in the back. He and Bella climbed in behind her. Roland made his appearance. "Since the house is now clean, Fred told me to drive you guys back to the motel. He and Devin will pack up the equipment. Devin was more shaken than hurt."

Jasmine merely nodded, she didn't feel like she had the strength to say anything as she leaned against Everit. His arm snaked around her as his body heat seeped into her bones. She didn't want to think of it, but she had to face facts, as weak as she was she thought she was dying. A tear slid out of her eyes as she thought of all the things she'd miss if she were.

Everit felt the moisture as it hit his hand. He knew what she was feeling, he'd been there himself when he went through his own change. It was time, but not at this moment she needed energy and sleep.

The SUV pulled into the motel's lot, and Everit passed the room's key to Roland. Roland's eyes grazed over Jasmine as he turned keeping his concern to himself. He pushed the key into the door a little forcefully. He didn't find this job interesting anymore. One of their members in the hospital, another hurt and the one they depended on the most seemed sick and getting sicker with each moment.

This wasn't funny anymore, it was getting worse in his opinion. If the boy Trevor weren't in danger, then he'd vote they just leave Westilville and let them deal with their own problem. But he couldn't do that, he wasn't that kind of person to let something so evil take the lives of children, and it hit him like a sledgehammer.

This dark entity was after the children. Most of the cases they'd investigated involved children. He passed the key back to Everit. "Sorry I can't stay, I'll bring the SUV back, but I have to talk to Fred right now." He trotted to the vehicle and hopped into the driver's seat and backed out of the parking slot and sped off into the night.

Everit shook his head as he placed Jasmine on the bed. Bella raced in behind them. "I'll walk you in a few, but first I need to tend to Jasmine." He reached into his pouch and pulled out the salve he always carries.

With gentle hands, he removed her shirt, boots, jeans and applied the salve to the scrapes and bruises. He checked her for broken bones then covered her with the blanket.

Jasmine couldn't fight the heaviness as her eyelids slid closed. Everit touched her temple and focused. This time the energy flowed through him at a quick rate, you could almost see it as his body glowed. Checking his own energy level, he allowed the flow to slow, and he was forced to stop it.

He turned to Bella who was his silent witness, "She'll be good as new tomorrow. Now, how about that walk."

Belle jumped up from her spot on the floor and bounded over as she jumped around him. Everit chuckled at her antics, "No wonder Jasmine chose you." He rubbed her head as he attached the leash to her collar, and led her out the door.

More images of strangers filled Jasmine's dreams. Each dream there was someone at the periphery she couldn't see the person but sensed that it was guiding her.

In the distance, she heard the door close, but she couldn't open her eyes to the noise. The pain from the scrapes and bruises had ebbed. She felt the bed bounce and shake for a moment. Then it creaked and moved as someone lay next to her. She immediately knew who it was, she could smell his scent, Everit. Her mind sighed.

He pulled her into his arms and whispered something Jasmine couldn't make out into her ear. Tomorrow? A corner of her mind wondered what was going to happen tomorrow? Would she still be alive tomorrow? Unshed tears collected behind her eyelids. Who would take care of Bella?

Everit heard her thoughts. He ran a hand through her hair until that part of her mind finally quieted and went to sleep too. She would need all her strength for tomorrow. He hoped she would accept her fate.

Chapter 16

Jasmine's eyes opened, and she looked over at the clock on the table. The numbers said it was twelve noon. Her eyes grew. Noon? What the heck, she threw the blanket back and stood up and glanced around. Neither Everit or Bella were there. He must have taken her for a walk, was all she could think of.

Her lips curved up in a smile, he was such a sweet man. No wonder she found herself attracted to him. She gathered some clothes, and for the first time, she glanced down at herself. The color drained out of her face as she practically screamed in terror. He'd undressed her last night, and she didn't remember it.

She wondered why she was so worried. Her mother that's why. She had enough trouble with Katie being the wild child what would she say if Jasmine did her own thing? Oh, she knew what her mother would say, she'd heard it enough. "Why can't your sister be more like you? Why can't she find a man her own age and stop running after older men?"

Mom didn't know everything, did she? Jasmine vowed she'd never know about Peter Mankiller. The only person who knew of the humiliation and abuse he put her through was Katie. She'd never told a soul and as far as she knew Katie had kept her secret.

Then Spencer slipped into her thoughts. He was like Peter, and he'd proved that he was just like her ex. Stop thinking about them, "Ugh... I need to stop thinking about them. Why do they invade my thoughts?"

She took a quick shower and dressed for the day. Then she grabbed a Coke out of the refrigerator and made herself some peanut butter crackers. She popped the top of the can and took a sip. She grimaced, it tasted funny to her, but she'd been sort of sick, which might explain the bouts of weakness she was having.

She quickly ate the crackers and drank the soda. As she cleaned up the table and got rid of her trash the door opened and Everit and Bella walked into the room. She turned and smiled at him she decided that he'd done right the night before and he hadn't tried to take advantage of her in her weakened condition.

Everit took the steps over to her, "How are you feeling?"

She closed her eyes as his strong hand caressed her cheek and she leaned into his touch. The callused skin suggesting a life that was used to hard work. She opened her eyes, "I'm better."

"We should go to the cave, there are some things I left behind," he didn't want to tell her here, but in a place where they could be alone. "You work so hard for others, but now it's time to take some time out for yourself." He let his arm fall to his side and waited for her answer.

She pulled out her keys and some cash from a bag just in case they needed to stop somewhere to get some food either along the way to the cave or back from the cave. She grabbed her cellphone and stuffed it into her pocket. She didn't think twice. If he needed something else, she'd help him get it. She didn't know why she felt such a kinship with him.

Maybe it was because they were both Native Americans living in a world that still didn't look kindly upon their people. It was like they were kindred spirits. Jasmine announced, "Okay, I'm ready."

Everit picked up a bowl and grabbed a couple of water bottles. "Just in case Bella needs something to drink. We should take her with us."

Jasmine smiled a second time. How thoughtful he was. She was beginning to think of him as the perfect man because of the way he knew what was needed. "Certainly."

They stepped out into the daylight and locked the door, and climbed into the Escape. Jasmine's cell phone rang, and she pulled it out of her pocket. Looked at the caller ID. Fred. She pressed the talk button on the screen. "Hey, Fred, what's up?"

"I saw you leaving was just thought maybe you could pick up Spencer. They're releasing him from the hospital."

Jasmine frowned but decided she'd go get the guy just to be free to go to the cave with

Everit. It wasn't a big cave, but it would be nice to get away for a while and not have to think about Spencer or anyone else for the rest of the day. Though she is still worried about Trevor and his family. "Sure, we can do that."

She turned to Everit after hanging up with Fred. "We have to go to the hospital and pick up Spencer. After we drop him off, we have the rest of the day."

Everit nodded, of course, it made sense to him. Fred had probably seen them climbing into the SUV. It was something he would have done and had done different times in his lifetime.

Spencer climbed into the Escape. "Has there been any progress on the cases?"

Jasmine nodded. She guessed that Spencer would ask this because he thought the team couldn't run without him. "We had a run in with the dark entity at Elijah Wilson's historical home last night. But Everit ran her away. Fred has some new information for you. You two need to talk." She pulled the SUV out on the road and drove to the motel.

Spencer leaned back in his seat. "Why can't you tell me?"

Jasmine sighed she didn't want to get into this now. "Because I'm taking the day off."

Spencer finally took a good look at her from the mirror. Her cheeks were hollower and thinner than usual, and there were dark circles under her eyes. She didn't look well at all. He wanted to tell her she needed to take care of herself but they would more than likely end in a fight. Finally, he just decided to drop it. "Okay."

Jasmine pulled the SUV into the motel's parking lot. Spencer climbed out, but he knocked on the window where Everit sat. Everit rolled the window down, Spencer leaned in and quietly said to him, "Take care of her."

Everit bobbed his head slightly. "I will." He pressed the button on the armrest on the door rolling the window back up as a mechanical whine came from the door.

Jasmine glanced over at him, "What was that all about?"

Everit smiled at her, "He wanted to make sure I take care of you."

Jasmine gaped at him. "He what?" She couldn't believe it. The man cared about how she felt? Well, that was a change. She shook her head to get the thought out of her mind. It was time to go take care of Everit's business.

She put the vehicle in gear and drove out of the parking lot. She drove down to the cemetery on Park Drive and pulled over to the side of the road. She slid out of the driver's seat, and Everit and Bella hopped out. The dog romped around in the grass by the cave and found herself a place to go. The heat of the day made it stifling and hard to breathe.

Everit led the way to the cave, and they stepped in. Bella found herself a comfortably cool space to lay down on and settled herself down as Everit moved to the back which was several feet away and pulled out a pack and what looked like a bedroll.

His fingers deftly untied the bindings on the bedroll, and he spread it out on the ground. Pulling open the pack he pulled out a candle and lit it, placing it on a rock and then he sat down and motioned for Jasmine to take a seat on the old buffalo robe.

Jasmine gazed at it. "A buffalo robe?"

Everit nodded, "Yes, I traded a horse to the Comanche for it. It was during the time I met a woman who traveled with them she was special, and I wanted to make her my wife, but she didn't feel the same way."

Jasmine sat down. Her curiosity was getting the better of her. He pulled out a flute, "This I learned to make when I lived with the Chickasaw for a while." He placed his lips to the flute and played a few notes, they were both sweet and sad sounding.

He stopped and placed the flute down beside him. "Jasmine, there was a time when I believed that I would find no one else to share my life with."

She cocked her head at him, was he proposing to her? Was he asking her to marry him? No way, she couldn't do that. She barely knew him, but there was something about him. Something in the back of her mind sparked.

Jasmine stared into his dark eyes, "What's happening between us?"

Everit held up his hand. "I should explain. Once a very long time ago there were a people who lived upon the land. They were people who could sense things, feel things, in the way we do. They were called Shadow People.

"They were a long-lived people who once the change came they tried to help their brothers and sisters of the human variety but there are always a few who are bad, and they found humans to be easy prey."

Jasmine sat straight up. Her brain trying to fit the pieces together, but it seemed so mind boggling to her. She opened her mouth to say something, but Everit stopped her by continuing with his story as he sat Bella's water bowl down near him and unscrewed the cap, pouring some of the water into the dog's dish.

"These people who preyed on humans actually exposed the Shadow People to humans. Although it is difficult to kill one, though they can be killed and the Shadow People were hunted mercilessly until they were almost exterminated. My mother was one of the last.

"She enjoyed killing, but I did not. I found I wanted to help my people but then the Spaniards came, and I fell ill. My mother stayed with me and then she told me the story on the day the change took place when I took my place as a Shadow Person."

Jasmine's mouth dropped, it clicked he was telling her she was one of these Shadow People, she would turn into a killer sucking the life from people. "No, I can't be," she whispered. Her mouth went dry as a lump formed in her throat.

She stood up and took a step back, as her voice rose. "No! I don't believe it! I won't believe it!"

Thunder crackled in the air, and she spun around as the sky grew gray.

Everit stood and reached out for her grabbing her hand in his. Her hand was clammy in his, he smelled her fear. "Jasmine, it's true. When the change comes, I want you here with me. You'll need an abundance of energy, and I'll be happy to supply it to you."

She shook her hand out of his grip and backed up another step. "Don't touch me! Don't come near me! I'm not a killer!"

Everit gazed at her, "I'm not either. Remember the day that Spencer yelled at you because he thought," he tried to remember the right word that the others had used, and his mind caught it, "you were a gold digger? I felt you through our link. I focused on him and only drained enough energy to make him sleep for a short while. I didn't harm him. I only wanted you to be happy."

Her eyes widened, and the blood ran out of her face. She glanced over to Bella who was laying now in the spot he'd vacated to stand near her. Bella trusted him. No, he's got to be lying. She had to get out of her get away and think things through.

She spun toward the entrance and ran out into the downpour that just started as the late July rain pelted her and plastered her clothes to her skin. She didn't know where she was going she ran past the SUV which looked inviting, but no she couldn't go there, he'd find her.

As the rain soaked into the ground, she skidded across the rain-soaked grass as she tried to stop to look around for a place to hide so she could think. Her thoughts were in such a mess she didn't see the headlights of the car slowing down, but then she flew as the bumper made contact and landed hard on the ground.

Jasmine shook her head as her mind tried to make sense of what just happened, but she couldn't focus. She groaned as she rolled over and saw the headlights blazing in her direction. She heard footsteps coming toward her as a person blocked the lights and a hand grabbed her by the arm, yanking her up to face the person she was most afraid of. Deputy Lewis James.

"Well, look what I just ran into," the man smiled at her with the mouth of a predator. He yanked her pulling her along to the car and not being gentle about it. He opened the car door, and shoved her in but deliberately smashed her head into the car's body. He pushed her into the seat. Reaching behind him he pulled out his handcuffs and cuffed her hands behind her back. Before he shut the door, he shoved her head smacking it forcefully into the dash. She thought she heard him say, "Lights out," then the slam of the car door.

She groaned and sat up when she felt the presence of him in the car next to her. She heard the door slam. The weakness was starting as her energy began to wane. No, not now, not here.

Deputy James, well by now-former deputy James leaned over to her as he pulled a knife out of a sheath at his belt. He held it in front of her face letting her see the blade and how big it was. "Now," he slid the knife back into the sheath, "we're going to go and have ourselves some fun." He shifted the car into gear and placed his foot on the gas as the vehicle lurched into motion. "Well, I'm going to have the fun," he amended, "as I carve you up into a bunch of little pieces no one will ever find."

Jasmine didn't want to leave anyone. Especially not Bella. A tear slid down her cheek. Maybe what Everit was telling her was true. She was finding it harder to stay with the here and now. She was going to die, and no one would know.

James drove his car into the woods and pulled up next to a tree where he knew a deer stand still stood once used by poachers. Of course, he'd caught the poachers in the act, and now they were doing some time in prison. But this bitch caused him his job. If he hadn't come up with his sob story about a woman who was dead, since he killed her himself, he'd still be sitting in jail awaiting his trial date. But he had plans. Kill the bitch, and then move on.

Everit could hear her thoughts as she ran out of the cave. He sat down and pat Bella's head. "She may come around." The dog seemed to understand, but several minutes later she stood up and shoved her head into Everit pushing him. She stared at him and moved to the cave entrance and turned and barked at him.

He thought she wanted to play, but her movements became more demanding. She ran over to him and put her jaws around his arm and pulled. She didn't apply enough pressure to break the skin or bite, but she was insistent.

He opened his mind that he'd closed to give Jasmine privacy, and saw the knife in front of her face, heard the words of Deputy James in his head. No, he wouldn't let it happen. He jumped up and glanced down at Bella for an instant, "Good girl." He raced out of the cave with his mind focused on Jasmine, just like the last time she was in danger. This time with Bella racing with him at his side.

James threw open his door tilted his seat up and reached behind it pulling the rope out he'd brought along for this. He slammed the door shut, crossed around the front of the car with the lights shining on a tree. He reached the passenger side, threw it open and grabbed

Jasmine by her handcuffed arm. He stopped as he saw a trickle of her blood running down her forehead. He put a finger to it and then popped it into his mouth. "Yum. Tasty."

Rain continued to fall, but the deluge slackened to a steady drizzle. Lightning flashed across the sky as thunder clapped off in the distance as the storm made its way to the south. The clouds thinned as the drizzle changed to a fine mist.

He yanked her over to the tree and propped her up against it and pushed her head back with force to stun her again as her head hit. He threw the rope over a low hanging branch and pulled it down and tied one end to the chain in the middle of the handcuffs and pulled her arms over her head. "Now this looks familiar," he grinned at her.

He pulled again as her toes barely touched the ground and she gasped in pain. Jasmine was so weak as he tied off the other end of the rope to another branch. She knew this was it, she couldn't fight back. She tried to struggle, but her energy was drained. James stepped in front of her and tapped the tip of the knife against his chin. "Where to start?"

He grinned at her and cut her shirt open. He tsked, "Such a waste, but you hurt me and then got me locked up so now I'm repaying the favor," he jabbed the knife into her shoulder.

Jasmine's eyes flew open, but she couldn't scream. He frowned, "This is no fun if you're not going to play along." He reached up, and from her wrist, he drew the knife down to her elbow. He sucked in a breath and yelled in her face, "Come on bitch, SCREAM!"

He jabbed the knife into her side. The closet to a scream she managed a moan he pulled the blade from her side with a sucking sound. She moaned as he stuck her again but in the other side. He reached out and smacked her across the face. "I want you to SCREAM!" he emphasized the last word and then punched her in the abdomen. Her stuck her in the abdomen, and that's when it happened. Something in her brain finally clicked. She felt hunger, one she'd never felt before. Her eyes focused on his and they glowed as his energy began to leave his body.

James tried to turn away but found he couldn't move. Something had him rooted to the spot. He couldn't look away found himself mesmerized by her eyes. Those brown eyes had a glow about them and fascinated him.

Heat ran through Jasmine's body as the energy surged and coursed through her. She felt her body starting to repair itself from the cellular level as the worst wounds knit themselves closed. It was a total rush. Now she understood, she was one of the Shadow People.

Jasmine heard crashing through the trees and Everit appeared with Bella at his side, but she didn't want to stop. She wanted to hurt the man who'd hurt her not once but twice.

Everit got in between James and Jasmine, but her focus wasn't on him it was on James.

She continued to drain him as if the Aztec wasn't there in front of her. "Jasmine, stop!" Everit stared into her glowing eyes. "Jasmine, don't become like my mother, it killed her." Finally, he did what he thought would stop the connection and he crushed his mouth onto hers and pulled her body to him as he kissed her.

Jasmine blinked, and her senses came back to her, and she found this man she was attracted to kissing her, and she responded in kind. As the kiss broke, she leaned her head onto him since she couldn't get loose from the rope tied to her arms. "I'm sorry. I'm so sorry I didn't believe you."

He reached up and untied her hands. James wasn't going anywhere he was too weak to move. Jasmine's arms lowered, but her hands were cuffed together. He now knew what a handcuff key looked like and he rummaged through James's pockets until he found them. Disgust raced through him at touching the man. He wanted to kick the former deputy who'd hurt Jasmine, but he didn't. He unlocked the handcuffs and let them drop on the ground.

He placed his arms around her as the clouds began to scud across the sky along with a gust of the summer breeze leaving the night sky with the moon shining down on them. She shivered in his arms. "I know where we can get dry."

Jasmine shivered again with another gust of wind. "I have to let the authorities know where he is so they can pick him up and revoke his bail. He'll never get out again."

She didn't realize her arm was dripping blood, she was so wet. She knew her cell phone wouldn't be usable right now. It was probably waterlogged. "Did you find a cell phone on him when you searched his pockets?" She looked up at Everit.

"No, I didn't." He stopped her, "I have to take care of your arm." He reached into his pouch and pulled out the cloth he'd used on her before and held it in the deepest part of the cut. Everit pulled out the pot of salve and dipped the cloth into it and with a gentle touch he rubbed it down her arm from wrist to elbow. He dabbed the cloth in a second time as a hint of blood ran from a small cut on her forehead. He scanned her for any more injuries and applied more of the salve to her bruises.

Jasmine walked over to the car which still ran and searched around inside trying to keep the events of her kidnapping from her mind, but they kept flashing in her mind. She opened the glovebox and found it laying on top of some papers. She unlocked it and dialed 911 she glanced over at Everit, "How did you find me?"

A woman came on the line. "What's your emergency?"

Jasmine quickly told the woman where she was at and that she was attacked a second time by former deputy Lewis James and where Sheriff Delmont could pick him up. She listened to the woman who told her to stay put because the Sheriff would have some questions to ask.

Jasmine sighed, "We have to stay until the Sheriff gets here."

Everit took his vest off and handed it to her, "Take off that shirt and put this on, it will give you some protection." He pointed at Bella, "She was insistent that something was going on. I had closed my link to your mind to give you privacy when I opened it again the only thing I saw was the knife and his voice. Both of us came to find you."

Jasmine removed the remnant of her T-shirt and slipped her arms into the vest. Even though it was a bit big the lining of the leather was warmer than the damp shirt. She buttoned it over her chest. He threw his arm around her waist and pulled her to him. She glanced over at Bella who stood over James in case he moved. Her fur was standing up, but she wasn't growing yet. Jasmine figured Bella would do that if James flinched. "Good girl."

Bella looked up once at her human and woofed. She bent her head back down to stare at the man who still lay on the ground like he was lifeless.

Twenty minutes passed as they stayed that way then saw the red and blue flashing lights through the trees. They heard people coming and saw Sheriff Delmont with a couple of his Deputies in tow.

Now it was time to come up with a believable enough story to keep the Sheriff and others from finding out they were in the presence of two Shadow People. Jasmine's muscles tensed as the enforcer of the law approached.

He motioned for one of the deputies to get James handcuffed. Bella moved away from the man's prone form on the ground and moved over to Jasmine and Everit taking a protective stance in front of her family.

Chief Delmont noticed the knife on the ground, the rope still tied off to the tree, and the handcuffs laying on the ground by the tree. "What's going on here?" His eyes narrowed at first thinking the two had taken the law into their own hands. Until he saw the bruises, the small cut on her forehead and the slice down her arm.

Jasmine trembled, she didn't want to think of what happened, but she had to tell him. So, told him her story as fast as she could. She twisted her fingers in her hands but told him that she and Everit had a fight and she ran out into the rainstorm. "And then Everit showed up, but James stumbled and fell he might have tripped over a wet root or something and hit his head. Everit freed me while Bella stood guard over him to make sure he stayed on the ground." She passed him the cut T-shirt as evidence.

Sheriff Delmont then questioned Everit, and he glanced over at Jasmine. "It was a stupid fight that we had. But somehow Bella here knew she was in trouble and wouldn't stop trying to drag me out into the rain. So, I followed her, and she led me here. That's when he saw us coming and tried to run."

The Sheriff eyed them both, but the dark and rain were going to make it hell to find physical evidence except the deputy he had bagged up the evidence called to him. "Hey Sheriff look at this." He pointed to the tree, and with his gloved hands, he pulled some hair from the trunk. "It's her hair, this must have happened when James smashed her head into the tree."

Delmont grunted and leaned forward and noticed a little bit of skin there too. "Bag the skin too." He turned toward the two. "Well, it looks like you're telling me the truth. This won't go well for James and this time he's going to stay in jail."

Jasmine's hands trembled as she placed her hands over her eyes and her knees buckled. She would have fallen if Everit hadn't pulled her up and gathered her into his arms. He whispered in her ear that it was okay. She pulled her hands from her eyes. "Thank you, Sheriff Delmont."

Delmont didn't know what to say, this young woman was kind even after everything done to her. He cleared his throat, "I'll have Deputy DuFrain take you back to your car."

DuFrain led them through the woods back to his car. He opened the rear door and Everit, Jasmine, and Bella climbed into the backseat. He shut the door and then climbed into the driver's seat. "Where can I take you?"

"We left our car over on Park Drive by the cemetery."

The man tilted his head up to look into the rearview mirror at them, "What were you doing there?"

Jasmine smiled up at him. "Exploring a cave."

The man took a second glance as he put his key into the ignition and cranked the engine over. "You two are part of the ghost hunters that are here, aren't you?"

Jasmine smiled at him and rubbed the fur on Bella's back. "Yes, we are."

The man continued driving and considered if he should tell them. He shrugged his shoulders and thought they looked like some nice people. "Well, the other night my son Timmy and a few of his friends snuck into the Wilson House. They heard about you and decided they wanted to try their own investigation. Timmy came running in the house that night nearly in tears. He said something scratched him on the back. Since then he's been plagued by nightmares. I got him to tell me today what he was up to. He showed me the scratches."

Jasmine leaned forward. The dark entity again. "Tell me what kind of nightmares?"

"He said he's chased through the woods and he falls into something then he comes face to face something dark and twisted, and a dog with red eyes attacks him and tries to rip his throat out. Then he wakes up. The odd thing is that before I left to go to work, I heard something growling. What does it mean?" He pulled the car over behind the black Ford Escape and turned around in his seat gazing back at the pair.

Jasmine considered what he said. This sounded similar to Trevor's haunting. "I believe your son is in danger, Deputy DuFrain and from something that wants to kill him for an event that happened over a hundred years ago."

DuFrain opened his door, and stepped out of the car and opened the back door letting the three out. "What can I do about it?"

Jasmine pondered his question, "Get your son out of the house. Look and see if you have any old journals or anything one of your ancestors might have written. I need to see them, find out if any entries date back to an event that happened that will lead me to the identity of the spirit haunting your son. Once I have that information I can fight it on my own ground."

DuFrain nodded, "How do I get hold of you if I find these journals?"

Jasmine looked around and saw his ticket book inside the car. She reached in, opened it, took his pen, and then wrote something down. "That's my phone number if you can't reach me then call the second number that's for Spencer Cross. Tell him, and he'll get word to me." She handed him his ticket book and pen.

Deputy DuFrain nodded and climbed back into his car and left. Everit went into the cave and grabbed his belongings and put them in the back of the SUV. Even though the air was muggy outside Jasmine ran the heater to keep the windshield from defogging as she drove back to the motel. She glanced at the dashboard clock and groaned. It was now one am. She pulled the SUV into the lot, and she and Everit slid out with Bella following.

Chapter 17

Jasmine didn't want to think about food right now she wanted to know more. Everit stepped up behind her and wrapped his arms around her and pressed a kiss to her neck. Jasmine leaned into him and let him nuzzle her neck, then he stopped at her ear. "We should eat and feed Bella."

She sighed, "Your right, but I didn't realize that Shadow People ate food."

Everit threw his head back and laughed as he released her. "Of course, we eat food. We have to keep our energy up, and the food is one way."

Jasmine rummaged around in the alcove. "We have some fruit, vegetables and peanut butter and crackers. I should go to the store tomorrow and get more food."

Everit eyed Jasmine, he knew she was brand new to be a Shadow Person, but even they could get sick, and he didn't like her color. It was off. "I'll take care of the food, you go get out of those clothes and into the shower before you catch a cold." Everit poured food and water into Bella's bowl. She crunched her food as they continued to talk.

Jasmine stared out of the alcove at him. "We can get sick, too?"

Everit's smile was gentle as he strode across the thin carpet. He placed a hand on her cheek, "Yes, we can. Even though we change, we are still essentially human."

Jasmine shivered again as the AC in the room clicked on. "Okay, but I need to know more about who and what we are."

Everit rubbed his thumb over her cheek. "I'll teach you." He leaned over and pressed his lips to hers. "Now, get out of those wet clothes."

Jasmine's eyes glinted as she smiled, mischievous glints in her eyes. "Okay, mother." She yelped then giggled as she evaded his grasp and heard him chuckle behind her as she ran to the bathroom. She stopped long enough to grab her sleep shirt and raced into the bathroom. In minutes she'd pulled off the damp clothes that wanted to stick to her skin and hopped into the warm shower.

Everit smiled. He walked over to the other bed and quickly stripped off his own wet clothes and rummaged around until he found the bathrobe that Jasmine had bought for him. He shrugged his arms into the terrycloth material and found the belt and tied it around his waist.

Walking over to the alcove, he pulled out a couple of apples, a selection of grapes. He pulled out his knife that he'd traded with a French trapper up in Canada over two hundred years ago and set to work slicing the apples. He wiped it off on his robe and replaced it in its sheath in his pack.

He listened to the water run in the bathroom as he quickly put together some peanut butter crackers. He put the plate on the table. This new world was strange, but he was getting used to it.

The water shut off and he grabbed two water bottles out of the refrigerator in the alcove and placed them on the table. He heard the blow dryer, and several moments later Jasmine stepped out in a matching robe.

She strode over to the table and took a seat in a chair near her. Everit glanced at her knowing she was full of more questions. "Not tonight, first we eat, then sleep, and then tomorrow I'll start answering all questions you may have when we're alone."

Jasmine sighed and propped her chin in her hand. "But I want to know more." Her gaze dropped to the table. "I can't tell the guys, they just wouldn't understand."

Everit reached out and took her hand in his, "No, you can't. You can't even tell your sister."

Jasmine brushed a stray lock of her strawberry blond hair out of her face. "I guess it's something I'll have to get used to. Being different that is."

He rubbed his thumb across her knuckles. "Jasmine you were always different from the day you were born. But you'll never be alone now." They ate until their hunger was sated. Everit stood from his chair and took her hand in his and pulled her up. He led her to the bed. Robes were removed, and they both climbed in.

He pulled her over cradling her as she lay her head on his chest.

Bella jumped on the bed and stuck her head in Jasmine's face. She stuck out her tongue and started licking the woman's face. Jasmine thought it was part of a dream until she smelled dog breath. Jasmine opened her eyes and shoved Bella's face out of her face, "Okay, okay. I'll take you out."

She glanced over at Everit and caught him peaking at her with one eye cracked open. She punched him in his shoulder. His muscles rippled as he rolled over and put an around her middle pulling her under him pinning her with his weight.

He pushed her hair out of her face and stared into her eyes. He lowered his face to hers and kissed her mouth, tentatively, she responded in kind. He kissed her chin, trailed kisses down her jaw to the ear. Jasmine moaned, but she fought off his seduction and placed her hands on his chest. "I told Bella I'd take her out."

He chuckled. "I did that earlier. You were sleeping so soundly I didn't want to wake you up." He nipped at her ear and nibbled on her neck as he stuck his hand up her T-Shirt. In a matter of minutes what little clothes she wore were removed. She wound her hands into his hair. She closed her eyes, she wanted him, yes, but she trembled. She was afraid.

He lowered his mouth to her ear, "Don't worry, I'll be gentle."

She closed her eyes expecting pain as he pushed into her. She gasped as the pain radiated between her legs, but he lay still for several minutes letting her adjust. As she grew accustomed, she pulled his face to her and kissed him deeply as she released her hold on his hand and ran her fingernails over his back. She kissed him again, now with her lips pressed to his, "Please."

Their bodies bonded in smooth and rhythmic motions. They twisted and turned exploring each other, and Jasmine knew this was the beginning of a better life for her, for them both.

They woke a couple of hours later, and Everit led her into the bathroom where they took another shower but after another round of sex. Jasmine was rejuvenated as they both dressed. She wore her favorite motorcycle boots, black skinny jeans and teal spaghetti strap stretchy tank. She noticed the slice in her arm was healed along with the bruises and the slit from having her head bashed into the dashboard. Everit dressed in his own boots, black jeans, white tank, and black vest.

Jasmine sighed found her phone wasn't working. "I guess it got too wet. I'll have to get a new cell, and you need one too."

Everit shrugged his shoulders. It didn't matter either way with him because he had no idea how to work the phone. As if she read his mind she bumped him with her hip, "I'll teach you silly."

"I'll hold you to that."

Someone beating on her door caught her attention as they pounded. "Has to be Spencer." She walked over to the door and pulled it open.

The first thing he noticed the rings under her eyes were gone and her cheeks looked fuller, much better than yesterday. "We're going to head to Elijah Wilson's house and meet with the curator."

"Okay, thanks for telling me. I should find a cell phone store. Mine totally died yesterday."

"What happened to it?"

Jasmine grimaced no way she was going to tell him the truth, she couldn't. He'd probably demand she make him one too, and she couldn't do that. He wasn't one of their people. "Got caught in a downpour yesterday and we got drenched."

Spencer reached for his back pocket. Jasmine waved both her hands at him. "You don't need to pay for it. I'll look for something for dinner tonight while we're out. And it might not be the best time to suggest this, but I think we should add Everit to the team."

Spencer pursed his lips and ran a hand through his blond hair. He glanced away from her. At first, it was going to be definite no as the little green monster of jealousy began to rear its ugly head. But after talking to Fred and listening to the recording of what happened at the Wilson house, he'd decided to ask Everit to join them.

His gaze returned to her face as her eyes searched his for a hint of a positive answer. "I was going to ask if Everit would join us. It makes sense to have two of you on the team. Besides asking about the meeting with the curator."

Jasmine turned to Everit. Her eyes fixed on his face as she waited for his answer. She hoped he would say yes.

Everit knew what his answer would be. He didn't want to be separated from her. He'd found someone, one of his own kind, who was willing to share her life with him. "Yes," his eyes lifted to Spencer's face. "I believe I'd be useful."

Spencer rubbed his hands together. "Good now that that's settled," he turned his attention back to Jasmine. "What are you going to do with Bella?"

Jasmine glanced around the leaned forward as if letting Spencer in on a secret. "I was hoping Roland or Devin would take her for me, so she doesn't have to stay in a hot car all day."

Spencer glanced down at Bella who stood next to Jasmine. "I think she has more fun with Devin."

Jasmine grabbed Bella's leash and attached it to her collar, she handed it to Spencer. "Oh, before I forget have you heard anything from a Deputy DuFrain?"

Spencer cocked his head at her. "No, should I have?"

Jasmine told him of their conversation with the deputy leaving out the other parts of her being kidnapped and tortured by former deputy James. A slight shudder ran through her.

Spencer nodded, "That agrees with Roland's theory that the dark entity is after the children of the descendants."

"I agree, and I want to find out who this dark entity was in life so we can permanently free this town. No child should have to live in fear."

Spencer turned with Bella in tow then stopped, "I'll let you know what we find out from the curator."

Jasmine beeped the lock on the Escape, "Thanks," she and Everit hopped into the vehicle. She stuck the key into the ignition and backed out of the slot. She stopped and glanced over at Everit. "When we get back, I want to hear some music from the flute."

Everit smiled at her. "Certainly."

She put the SUV into gear and pulled out of the parking lot into the flow of traffic. If she remembered correctly the cell phone place was down on main near Jackson Street.

They emerged from the store. Jasmine with her new phone but with the same number. She was a little aggravated that the salesperson had said that she should have put the phone in rice right after. Easy for the girl to say, but when Jasmine didn't have any rice around what was she to do especially when no stores were open at one a.m.

She bought Everit a simpler phone. One of the older androids that were easier to use. He stuffed his phone into his pouch.

Jasmine glanced over at the pouch resting on his hip, "What do you carry in there?" Curiosity getting the better of her.

Everit leaned in and gave her a quick peck on the cheek, "You'll see in time," he smiled as they walked toward the SUV.

Jasmine rolled her eyes. "Be evasive," she climbed in the SUV and slammed her door shut.

Everit climbed on the passenger side and turned to her. "I'm entitled to keep some secrets to myself just as you entitled to your secrets."

Jasmine stabbed the key into the ignition. "I agree, but I thought we were a couple now. If we are then, we shouldn't have any secrets between us. Because I've learned the hard way that secrets are a good way to destroy any relationship."

Everit reached out and grabbed her hand in his. "Jasmine, I have lived a very long life and most of the time in societies where certain things were kept secret. Which is just how it was done." He paused and swallowed. This new world with new rules could be frustrating. "This is all new to me. So, when I'm ready to share, I will. But I must start your training as soon as possible."

Jasmine's facial muscles went slack as she stared back at him. "Training? What training?"

He lifted her hand to his face and kissed the knuckles. "I need to teach you how to spiritually heal a person. We should start with Spencer first since he had a spirit possess his body. This makes him vulnerable to being possessed again."

"So, we did didn't totally free him from Virgil Bartlet's spirit?"

Everit leaned over to her his face and tone very serious. "There's always going to be something that lingers from possession. We have to make sure there's nothing left."

"How do I do this?"

"I'll teach you how."

Jasmine's stomach rolled as she tasted a sourness in her mouth. Could she find a place to hide? No, she knew from experience she wouldn't be able to hide from him. He'd find her no matter where she disappeared too. "Why can't you be the one to do this?"

Everit couldn't help but grin at her. She amused him at this moment. "I can do it, but don't you think we should have two people on the team who can spiritually heal others. I mean if I had an attachment wouldn't it make sense if you knew how to remove it."

Jasmine stared at him she knew her answer to his question. Knew it in the pit of her stomach, "Yes, I would. I wouldn't want to see you or anyone I know and care about harmed by anything."

He'd known that would be her answer, he just had to make sure that she knew too. "Let's go down to the park in the town center, and I'll explain the process."

Jasmine started the Escape and pulled out into traffic and drove down to the center of town. She found a place to park. The bright sunlight promised another hot one today without a cloud to provide even a few minutes of relief. She shut off the engine, and they climbed out of the vehicle and strode across the grass to the park. They stood under a tree which provided some shade.

She glanced at him as a breeze blew that stirred his dark black shoulder-length hair. She saw the warrior that was hidden within and could imagine how he'd look astride a horse, riding with the plains tribes and how at home he would have been in buckskins as he was when she first met him. The vision stirred the woman within her.

Again, he seemed to know what she was thinking as he turned to her, a smile tugging at his lips. He brushed her hair out of her face then turned back to look at the families moving around the park. "As you know, everything that's alive has a life force. That life force gives off energy."

Jasmine nodded. "An aura."

"What I want you to do is see the aura."

She focused hard on the people and children running around the park. She couldn't see it no matter how hard she focused. "I can't do this." Her voice cracked, as her head dropped and she stared at the ground feeling like an utter failure.

Everit placed a hand under her chin and tilted her head up. "You're not. You don't use your eyes for this you use your mind. You have to reach out with your mind and see the aura," he tapped her forehead. "Now close your eyes and see this park with your mind."

Jasmine closed her mind and could feel his mind with their psychic connection. She heard his voice in her mind. "Remove the barriers you have in place and open your mind."

Her hands grew clammy as her shoulders tightened. She lowered her voice to a whisper, "I'm afraid. I've kept the voices out for so long."

Everit knew what she was talking about. The voices of other people's minds could be so strong, and they never knew they were projecting their thoughts into the minds of people who could hear them. People like himself and the woman next to him. He took her hand in his, "I'm here. I'm with you."

She held onto his hand tightly as she lowered the barriers. She focused on the scene before her as she concentrated and finally she saw. It was so obvious people moved around her and Everit as their aura's glowed brightly. She heard his voice in her mind. "These are people who have never had an attachment. Their auras glow bright, brighter than sun especially with the children."

"I never knew. I mean you can see an aura on a photograph, but I didn't know you could see them like this."

Everit gave her hand a squeeze. "A person with an attachment their aura will be dull looking not as bright, and you'll see something if it lingers is something dark attached to it that could look like a dark black root."

Jasmine nodded, "How would I remove it if I saw it?"

Everit spoke out loud this time as he moved closer to her. "You'd envision the sage as a weapon, something easy for you like a knife and use the smoke to cut through the root, and then heal the cut with the sage."

Jasmine gasped as she gripped his hand harder. "What's that?" She pointed in her mind towards a piece of ground that had something black almost like a tiny tendril moving across the ground.

Everit growled, "It's the dark entity, she's looking for something or someone. I'll stop her." He released Jasmine's hand and strode purposefully across the grass to the place where he mentally saw the piece of the dark entity. It reminded him of a root. Quietly he chanted, pulled out some white powder and sprinkled it on the ground. He heard the entity scream in his mind, furious that she was stopped again.

He stood and crossed the grass to Jasmine. "It's done. She won't return here again."

"You're sure it's a she?" She had to wonder if it was male pretending to be female to throw them off.

Everit wrapped his arms around her, "Yes I am," he lowered his mouth and kissed her deeply. They broke apart when they heard a throat clearing noise near them and turned to face the person.

Deputy DuFrain stood there, and in his hand, he carried two leather bound books that looked very old. "I hope this will help," he said as he held them.

Jasmine took them from him reverently as if they were holy books. "Thank you Deputy DuFrain, I'll return them when I'm finished with them."

DuFrain shook his head. "Just give them to my brother, Marcus. He's the curator of Elijah Wilson's house." He smiled, gave them a lopsided grin. "Please call me Andrew," he tipped his hat and ambled off toward the Sheriff's office.

Everit ran his hand down Jasmine's back, "We should pick up whatever you wanted to get for tonight and head back to the motel. I can see by that look in your eye you want to dive into the journals."

She grinned up at him. "You're such a mind reader."

Everit chuckled as he led her back to the Ford. "I don't have to be a mind reader in this instance. I can see it in your eyes."

Chapter 18

They loaded the purchases from the grocery into the Ford. She'd bought the guys some more snacks and bought several things for dinner upon Everit's suggestion. They drove back to the motel and parked. Jasmine saw Devin walking Bella. She walked over to the space that separated the buildings and cupped her hands around her mouth. "Hey Devin, we're back."

Devin glanced up, and both he and Bella ran over to Jasmine. "What all did you get?"

Jasmine smiled as she led them over to the motel room, "Stuff."

They entered the room as Everit collected some items out of the bags that he would cook out on the charcoal grill. Jasmine stuffed some items in a bag and passed it over to Devin. "Just more snacks."

Devin grinned at her. "You spoil us too much, but don't stop."

"When you go back tell the others that I have some stuff for them, too." She smiled at Devin but really, she was using her new-found power to examine their auras. She had to make certain that each one was clean.

Devin stepped out of the motel room with a bag in hand. Jasmine filled other bags and knelt in front of Bella as she rubbed a hand along the dog's fur from head to mid-back. "Did you have fun with Devin, today?"

Bella woofed at Jasmine, and then stood up and shoved her body into Jasmine's with her tail wagging. Jasmine laughed. "Don't worry I didn't forget about you." Jasmine stood and rooted through a bag and pulled out a ball. She tossed it gently, and Bella took a few steps catching it. She lay down on the carpet satisfied as she tried to crush the ball between her powerful jaws.

Everit stepped over to her and pressed a kiss to her lips, "I'll be outside getting the grill ready."

Jasmine smiled at him and wrapped her arms around him hugging him. "A progressive. I like that."

He smiled back. "I don't know what that means, but I've always helped my wives."

Jasmine let out a shocked mock gasp. "Breaking with the tradition of the warrior and hunter." She let out a peal of laughter. "I'm teasing."

Everit smirked at her, "I know." He strode out of the motel room. He liked cooking over a campfire, but the grill would work just as well. He put the charcoal on the grill, and even though he wasn't there when Jasmine had lit it, he knew how it was done. He'd followed her with his mind as he slept that day.

He put the right amount of lighter fluid on it then lit the charcoal as Fred and Roland came out of their rooms and came down the stairs.

Fred moved over to him, "I thought Jasmine was going to do this. At least, that's what Spencer said earlier."

"Well, I decided to give her a break. She's been through a lot and needs to rest."

Fred clapped a hand on Everit's shoulder. "You're a good man." Roland seconded that comment. Then Fred pointed toward the motel room. "Is she up?"

"Yeah, she insisted on getting something for all of you." He chuckled. "When she's like that there's no stopping her."

Fred motioned for Roland to follow him to the room. Fred knocked on the door, and Jasmine opened it. As she turned to the table, she did a quick scan over the pair and was satisfied that both of their auras were good.

Jasmine handed them their bags, and the pair hurried out. Noting that Jasmine looked better, but they both saw a tiredness in her eyes. As if her energy level was running low.

"Thanks, Jasmine," Roland grabbed Fred and drug him out of the room. They stopped by Everit for a minute. "You need to make her get some rest, she's practically dead on her feet."

Everit grimaced at Roland's colorful use of words. "I will don't worry." Several moments later Spencer slipped out of his room and strode past Everit. Something didn't seem right to Everit. Spencer didn't stop to even try to chew the fat as the others had and the grill needed another thirty minutes before it would be ready to go. Everit rose from his chair and silently Spencer to the motel room that the blond man had just stepped into.

Jasmine quickly scanned Spencer, and she saw it in her mind. The sick looking aura and the root, but there was something else there. She opened her eyes and turned around. Spencer's eyes were totally black again, and his smile was feral. Bella jumped up and growled at him and started barking furiously.

Jasmine stared back at Spencer, "Get out of him Virgil." She hoped Spencer could hear her. "Spencer, fight him. Virgil is still inside you."

Spencer shook his head, and his eyes returned to normal, and he sagged for a moment. Jasmine grabbed him and supported him as she unlocked the door. "What happened?"

"Virgil Bartlet still has a hold on you. I have to get him to release his hold so I can heal your aura."

Spencer craned his head as Everit opened the door he stood up straight and wrapped his hands around Jasmine's throat. "You will not get rid of me. I like this body," Virgil's voice came out of Spencer's mouth as he squeezed.

Jasmine felt her air supply being cut off. She locked eyes with him as her face turned a sickening purple. Her eyes started to glow, and the grip on her neck started to loosen. She broke the contact as she gulped air in. "Spencer," she croaked, "fight him."

Everit rushed over and grabbed the blond man from behind pinning his arms behind his head. "Get the sage, he's still too strong." Everit fought to stay on his feet as Spencer struggled to get out of the grasp.

Jasmine lit the sage and closed her eyes seeing the connection which was on Spencer's chest. She heard Everit chanting as she envisioned the sage as a knife and began to sever the connection. She continued until the last connection was gone. It tried to reconnect, but she forced it away with the sage. Then she envisioned Bartlet being consumed by the smoke, they both heard a scream, and he was gone.

Everit released Spencer who'd stopped struggling and Jasmine stubbed out the stick. Bella's frantic barking stopped.

Spencer glanced at the two of them, then noticed the vicious dark bruises coming up on Jasmine's neck. "The last thing I remember was you telling me that Virgil Bartlet was still connected to me."

Jasmine nodded and took another gulp of air.

Everit clapped Spencer on the shoulder. "I knew something was wrong so I tried to get in but the door was locked."

"I remember Jasmine had just unlocked the door and then I can't remember anything."

"Virgil tried to kill her using you," Everit was calm as he spoke. This could shake Spencer to his core if it weren't handled right.

Jasmine glanced up at Spencer. "Everit stopped you, and I severed him from you.

You're now free of Bartlet. He'll never bother you again."

Spencer pulled a chair out from the table and let his body sink down in the chair. He held his head in his hands as he realized he'd made a major mistake. How could I have let it get this far, he thought as he glanced towards the bed.

Everit with a hand wrapped around Jasmine's waist helped her lay down on the bed. He pulled a small clay pot out of his pack and rubbed the ointment on Jasmine's neck. He bent over her and pushed some hair out of her face. "Rest now. I'll come get you when it's time to eat."

Spencer was taken aback by how gentle he was with her. Gentle and loving like a lover came to mind. Everit caught the other man's eye and pointed toward the door. The two men stepped outside, and Everit strode over to the grill checking the condition of the charcoal. He reached into the cooler by him that held the food he would cook and shoved it out of the way pulling out a drink he passed it to Spencer. He indicated Spencer should sit in a chair.

Spencer sat down and unscrewed the cap to the bottle of water and drank deeply. The cold water chilled his throat as the coolness slid down to his stomach. He sat the bottle down on the arm of the lounge chair. "Thank you."

Everit stared off into the distance for a moment, "No need to thank me. You looked like you needed it." He turned to gaze at Spencer's face. The man's emotions were written all over his face. Sadness, a hint of jealousy, and maybe a hint of grief. "Spencer, don't let what happened to stop you from what we do. As a leader, you require the utmost skill and professionalism of the team. That I've seen firsthand. I will do my best to live up to your expectations, but we also look to you to be your best too."

Spencer nodded, but he frowned as he stared at the coals starting to glow on the grill. Everit rose and began putting the food on the grill so it would start to cook. Spencer glanced at the other man who worked at preparing their food. "How can I do that when I get possessed by an evil spirit?"

Everit turned to the man. Time for a few simple truths. "You were angry that day, but I believe that was Virgil Bartlet's doing. He looked for a person who was weakened, and you allowed your emotions to give him a way in. This is where it's difficult to keep your emotions at bay. Once he got in, he was able to influence you until he took control."

Everit turned back to the food, and once he was sure it was going to cook evenly, he returned to his seat. He chuckled at a thought and turned to Spencer. "Jasmine is an important part of this team being she knows a lot about getting rid of entities. This is why Virgil Bartlet targeted her today. Because she forced him to leave the last time. However, you can see the strain this one is putting on her. She has to be allowed time to regain her strength." He left out the fact that the change didn't help matters any.

Spencer nodded, "I can understand that." He grinned as he turned to Everit, "She's sort of like the mother hen to all of us. Tries to make sure we eat good food while we're on a case."

Everit grinned back, "I know that first hand. She made me rest." He pursed his full lips for a moment. "This mayor needs to realize that for someone like her she needs to recharge. It may take a couple of days."

Spencer had never thought about it this way. Jasmine was always so strong. He had to wonder if this job was taking too much out of her. Maybe he should ask her to step down from the team.

Everit could sense Spencer's thoughts. One of the gifts of his kind. "No, what your thinking would hurt her even more. This is a job she likes, as much as she does with her business. Don't take that away from her."

Spencer's eyes widened, "How did you know?"

Everit smirked at the other man. "I'm the same as Jasmine, and I can read people maybe better than she can."

Spencer found that working with psychic mediums had advantages. "So, what happened in there earlier with Virgil Bartlet? Is he really gone, he won't come back to haunt me?"

Everit's head bobbed, "Yes, he's gone. He won't return." He needed to discuss this with Spencer. "Did you find anything out from the curator at the Wilson house?"

"Not really just some vague references to someone the law was trying to apprehend."

Everit's dark eyes turned to Spencer. "Deputy DuFrain found two journals that he gave to Jasmine earlier today. She wants to dig into them, but I'd like to pass them to you. I'd like to take her someplace tomorrow to just relax for a day."

Spencer nodded, he knew she needed a break. He swallowed hard and found it difficult, but he needed to let her go. After seeing the way Everit had tended to her, he knew there was no way he would have any kind of sexual relationship with her. He finally gave voice to what he thought. He picked up the bottle and turned it around in his hands, "I take it you and Jasmine are a couple now."

Everit's answer was simple and to the point. "Yes, we are."

Spencer's mouth went dry, and he found it difficult to swallow. "I've seen she does all the driving."

Everit's smile was slightly grim. "I can't drive."

Spencer nodded, again. "Don't do what I did and hurt her. I ruined my chances, and I see that now." Spencer held up a finger, "But I'd like for you two to take Devin with you tomorrow, in case Jasmine gets tired is all. Devin adores Bella, and he can keep her occupied."

Everit gazed into Spencer's eyes. He saw that the blond man meant what he said. "Okay, we'll take Devin with us."

Spencer rose from the chair, "Can you give me those journals so I can get started on them tonight," he smiled at Everit. "Thanks for the water and the talk."

A half-hour later Everit decided the dinner was finished. He strode toward the motel room he shared with Jasmine and Bella. He didn't want to wake her and Bella lay next to Jasmine lifted her head and stared at him. He picked up the journals and motioned for Bella to stay where she was. He turned and walked out.

Carrying the journals, he walked to Spencer's room and knocked on the door. It was pulled open. Everit held up the journals. Spencer took them from him. "We can get on them right away."

"Eat first, work later."

Spencer chuckled. "You sound like Jasmine."

Everit twisted his face into a smirk. "I suppose talking about her earlier made me realize that it's good to remind your friends to eat."

Spencer frowned, he got the message to either eat or deal with an angry Jasmine later. He did not want to face her wrath. He sat the journals on the table in his room. "Let's go eat," he knocked on Devin's door. "Get Fred and Roland, tell them it's time to eat."

He and Everit walked over to the grill. There was grilled chicken, grilled salmon, grilled corn on the cob, and potatoes. Spencer picked out what he wanted and grabbed a soda out of the cooler, and he sat down to eat.

Everit turned as Bella came bounding out of the motel room. Jasmine followed her. Everit wrapped an arm around her. "I wanted you to sleep longer."

Jasmine looked away a moment, "Nightmare." She wrapped her arms around him and just held on.

Roland and Fred descended the steps while Devin looked down from the balcony and slapped his hands on his face. A yelp ripped out of his throat as his eyes widened and he lowered one hand from his face and pointed at the pair below in between the buildings.

Roland stomped back up the steps, "Are you, nuts man. So, they're a couple now. So, what." He wanted to shake the man in front of him.

"But… what will this do to Spencer?"

Roland glanced down at everyone. Spencer was relaxed. "It's not bothering Spencer so get over it and join us. It's not every day we get a good meal while out on a job."

Devin tried to relax, but his stomach was roiling. He was worried about Spencer. He'd seen firsthand what low morale had done to the man and this might put him over the edge.

Spencer crooked his finger, and Devin stepped over to the man. "Look, this is new to me too, but I now realize that Jasmine should be happy. Everit makes her happy, so that's it. I'm stepping back and will let her be happy."

Devin felt his guts loosen as Fred with a plate in hand sat in a chair next to Spencer. "It's a very adult thing to do," Fred smiled and nudged Spencer in the ribs with his elbow.

The blond man looked up at Devin as the sun sank behind some trees. "Tomorrow you're going on a ride with Everit and Jasmine. He wants to take her somewhere, and I agree she needs some time to rest. I didn't realize this until Everit explained it to me. This job can take a lot out of a person, and Jasmine has been giving us at least one hundred and ten percent. It's time we do the same for her."

A slow smile appeared on Devin's face. He finally understood, not only was Spencer concerned with Jasmine's happiness but her health also. "Okay."

"You are to keep Bella occupied, and then you drive back, no need to put more pressure on her."

Roland grinned at them. "Good, I don't want to see any more of his," he poked Devin with a finger, "impersonations of the kid from Home Alone. That was just scary." He shuddered as he sat down in a chair. He lifted his head, "Hey, lovebirds, you need to eat."

A round of laughter broke out. Jasmine pulled away from Everit as the color drained out of her face and she gazed at the others. She didn't realize they were all there, Spencer included.

Spencer stood up from his seat and did something no one else expected. "I know this isn't a glass of wine, but…" he raised the can of soda he was drinking, "to Jasmine and Everit, may you be happy together." He brought the can to his lips and took a sip of soda and sat back down to finish his meal.

Everit stepped up behind Jasmine putting his hands on her shoulders, and he applied light pressure. She heard his voice inside her mind, "He means it."

A small smile curled her lips. "Thank you, Spencer."

Spencer waved it away. "Fred and I have some work to do tonight, but everyone else can do whatever they want. But tomorrow is a free day for Jasmine, Everit, and Devin. I expect we'll be dragging Roland in to check with Marcus DuFrain at the Wilson house on anything we discover from those journals."

Jasmine sat down on the lounge chair near Spencer, "But I thought I was going to go through those journals."

Spencer gazed into her brown eyes. "Not this time. You do a lot for us on our investigations. I never saw that before. But now that I do, it's time we stepped up to the plate and did our share."

She looked over at Everit who winked at her. He'd said something to Spencer. She didn't know to be angry or happy he did it.

Bella sat down next to Jasmine looking for a hand out. Jasmine pulled off some chicken meat and passed it to her dog who greedily gulped the treat down.

Devin finished his plate, threw away his garbage and picked up the frisbee. "Hey, Bella, want to play?" Bella woofed as Devin tossed the frisbee and she gave chase. A grin stood out on his face.

Sweat beaded Jasmine's forehead even as the breeze blew. It was still hot as the sun sank further down past the horizon. She glanced up as light gauzy clouds passed overhead. Stars appeared in the purplish-blue sky as the sun painted the clouds with reds, oranges, and yellows.

Fireflies flashed, blinking like warning flashers as they flew lazily over the ground. Mosquitos buzzed, and crickets and grasshoppers chirped. Somewhere in the distance, a bull-frog added to the symphony of light and sound.

Everit picked up her now empty plate and tossed the waste into a garbage can. He took her hand in his, and she stood. He led her behind the building, and he looked out towards the north-west. "About ten miles or so from here is the Shawnee village where I was headed when the quake struck. I'd like to see if it still exists."

Jasmine glanced away. *Of course, he'd want to know what might have happened to his wife. I guess under similar circumstances I'd want to know myself.*

Everit knew she understood, "Yepa was a fine woman. I hope she didn't wait for long for me to return and went on with her life."

Jasmine turned to face him and placed a hand on his cheek, "You have me now. I know we just met, but I don't know if this makes sense, but I love you."

Everit smiled and wrapped his arms around her pulling her to him, "As I love you too." He hugged her tightly, "I just need to know." He loosened his grip and then stared down at her face. "In the past, I would ask the father to grant me permission to take his daughter for my wife and give him a gift of wealth that I owned. Then the father would give us his blessing usually followed by a feast and then our wedding night. How is this ritual done in this day?"

Jasmine giggled, "nowadays it's usually customary to ask the girl and then present her with a ring. Set the date after a reasonable time, invite the family and guests, get married by a priest, followed by a dinner, then the honeymoon."

Everit crushed her to him again, "Sounds too complicated."

Jasmine smiled, "I'm sorry, but that's how marriages are conducted here. Although, we can just live together like we're doing now and not worry about marriage."

"Then we'll do that."

Jasmine let her head drop, and her strawberry blond hair fell about her face. She knew she was happy, but she couldn't help the uncertainty over the choice she made. It was like her brain kept over analyzing this new place she was at. If she were right, she'd watch her parents, her sister, everyone she cared about grow old and die around her, but she would never age.

Everit sensed her confusion. "It will be okay. When they are more accepting, know us better we'll tell them. But not today, or tomorrow, but sometime in the future."

Jasmine wrapped her arms around him and put her head on his chest. "Just hold me. Never let me go."

Everit stroked a hand through her soft hair. "I'll never let you go."

Chapter 19

Jasmine dressed in her favorite boots, blue jeans, and T-shirt. She drove the black Ford Escape down a back road following Everit's directions. He was in his buckskins and moccasins. Devin sat behind them in a Metallica T-shirt, jeans, and tennis shoes. Bella lay on the seat beside him with her head resting in his lap.

Everit looked up at a bridge that crossed the Apple river. It was surrounded by several trees, tall grass, with a small town to the north. "Here it was."

He glanced around him seeing in his mind the village that stood here with the wigwams built from the bark of trees and mud, smoke coming from cook fires, the women working in the fields where they grew the food while men went out to hunt. He could see the central meeting house, bigger than the smaller family buildings.

He saw her, well not the physical sense but the woman he knew now in spirit form still working in the field, with a small bundle strapped to her back. He climbed out of the vehicle and took the steps through the grass where their home would have stood.

The woman stood and turned to stare at him. Her spirit glowed with purity. "Everit," she ran over the grass and slammed into him.

Everit gazed at her nothing about her hand changed. "Your home."

Everit's smile held sadness. She hadn't moved on, she was the same woman he had left to go out trapping that summer of 1810 and work his way down the Mississippi River. He started back home in the fall, but the harsh winter had slowed him down. Finally, he sought shelter in the cave when the first earthquake struck.

Yepa stepped back from him. Her smile held a shyness to it which was why he fell in love with her in the first place. "I want you to meet someone," she pulled the carrier off her back. "Meet your son, Ouray."

He looked down at the child, "Arrow." The infant had large brown eyes, and a small tuft of black hair grinned up at Everit. He'd had a son he never knew. One who would always be this small and never grow old. He asked himself what had happened to them. He closed his eyes to search out the truth. Then he saw it the sickness, Smallpox. She was sick with it, but she tended Ouray who was so tiny, so small. His son died first, followed by Yepa two days later.

His eyes watered as his arms hung down at his sides. His voice cracked, "I'm sorry, I tried to get home to you and our son. I wish I could have been here." He broke down into sobs as he sank down to his knees, a rock dug in supplying pain that he knew he deserved. He held his hands skyward. He sang his song of grief and pain as he hoped the lord and the queen of the underworld would hear him and grant peace to his wife and child.

A bright light, brighter than the sun flashed near him. Everit swallowed, it was the lord of the underworld himself, Mictlanteutli who walked over to Everit. "I grant your prayer. They will be safe with us, and will never be in pain ever again, Acalan."

Everit nodded, he was surprised to hear his given name spoken by the lord of the underworld. As the light disappeared so did Yepa and Ouray. He sat back on his heels, and his chin hung down to his chest as his tears ran down his face.

Devin leaned forward looking out the windshield. "Uhm... Is he okay?"

Jasmine fought to control her own emotions and allow Everit some time to deal with his grief. She cleared her throat. "Yes, he will be." In time, she knew he would be fine.

Jasmine turned around in the driver's seat. "Drive us back, okay?"

Devin was going to drive back anyway, "Change of plans?"

Jasmine turned back around as she opened the driver's door, "Yes." She slid out and closed the door behind her. Her steps were tentative as she walked over to where he knelt. She didn't know what was said, but she saw what happened.

She stopped in front of him not sure if he wanted her there at that moment when his arms wrapped around her middle and he pressed his head to her stomach. He allowed his tears to flow a little longer before he finally released her and stood up.

Everit gazed into Jasmine's eyes. "We had a child, Ouray, she named him since I wasn't here." He looked over the overgrown ground, the tall blades of grass that had gone to seed. "They died of smallpox."

Jasmine gazed into his dark eyes, "I'm sorry." She put her arm around him and let him lean on her as she led him back to the Ford. Bella hopped out of the seat and jumped up front with Devin. Jasmine helped Everit climb into the vehicle, and she climbed in after him. It was her turn to help him.

Devin pulled the Escape into the motel parking lot as Roland was ready to leave for the second time that day to corroborate some information that Spencer and Fred had come across.

Roland rolled his window down. "That was a short trip. I thought you were going to be out all day."

Devin shook his head and then mouthed that it wasn't the time to ask. Roland glanced towards the back and saw the way Jasmine held Everit like a mother comforting a child. Devin pulled over to the second building and parked the vehicle into the slot allotted for their motel room. Before getting out Devin looked up into the rearview mirror, Everit's eyes were red. "I'll take Bella with me for a while if that's okay."

Jasmine glanced up at Devin, her eyes were soft as they filled with tears. "Thank you." She pushed open the door and slid out then helped Everit out of the Escape and into the motel room. She stepped back out and grabbed his pack and retrieved her keys from Devin as he led Bella to the first building.

She stepped inside the room and found him sitting on the side of the bed. She strode over to him and knelt in front of him taking his moccasins off. She tugged his buckskin shirt off over his head. She crawled across the bed and propped herself up on the pillows.

Everit lay down and put his head in her lap. She ran her fingers through his thick black yet silky shoulder-length hair. She couldn't think of anything to say that would help him with the grief of knowing not only had his wife but his child had died. So, she just hummed quietly hoping the tune would soothe him. He closed his eyes and listened quietly.

She heard a knock on the door, and Spencer strode in. The first thing he noticed was that the bruises on Jasmine's neck had faded to almost nonexistent. The second thing was that she was comforting the man in her life. Jasmine held up a finger to her lips as she hummed.

He walked around to where she sat on the bed. "Devin said you'd returned early."

Jasmine nodded, "Something came over Everit," she wasn't about to tell him that she'd watched as he sent his wife and child to the spirit world and was not only grieving but also felt guilty for not being able to get back home to them.

"It's good you two came back. I'm going to call a team meeting tonight and discuss how we can get rid of this dark entity. Do you think he'll be up to it?"

Everit sat up, and Spencer startled took a quick step back. "Don't worry, I'll be fine."

Spencer eyed Everit as if seeing him for the first time. The muscles that rippled across his chest and his arm muscles that were twice as big as Spencer's. Spencer was physically fit, but this was someone he could only compare to the Rock. Although Everit wasn't as muscular as the Rock, he was close.

Spencer couldn't think of anything else to say other than, "I hope to see you both at the meeting. We're going to Cracker Barrel."

Jasmine rolled her eyes, and her sarcasm wasn't lost on Spencer as she said, "Great…"

"Be ready to go," he looked down at his watch, "by seven." He spun on his heel and walked to the door. "Don't be late." He stepped through the doorway and shut the door behind him.

Jasmine stood up a moment and then she just flopped back down on the bed, "Why the hell do I bother…." She stared up at the ceiling. Then she glanced over at Everit who chuckled. She lifted her torso up on her elbows. "What is so funny?"

Everit's eyes were turning back to normal but were bloodshot, "You are. You worry about everyone else but yourself." He was glad he'd found her and that she was one of his kind. He leaned over her and claimed her mouth with his as his hand slid up under her T-shirt. He ended the kiss then propped his head up on his elbow as he gazed into her brown eyes. "Thank you, for understanding."

Jasmine rolled over onto her side and propped her head on her elbow. She placed a hand on his strong muscled chest and felt his heart. "Yepa and Ouray will live forever in your heart, I know that and I would never make you try to forget them."

Everit placed his hand over hers. "They all reside in my heart, all the time I spent with them and my children. I moved on and started new again, but I always tracked them down years later to make sure they were happy. Now Yepa and Ouray are finally at peace, and a piece of them lives on in me."

Jasmine gazed at him, this man so gentle, so kind, so caring, her heart swelled and beat strong for him. He released her and snaked his arm around her waist and pulled her to him.

Everit's mouth was on hers, demanding. Jasmine responded in kind. At that moment he needed her more than he needed anything before. Clothes removed, their bodies became as one.

Chapter 20

They lay together, sweat glistening off their bodies. They both dozed but awakened as someone banged on the door to the motel room, the pounding insistent.

Jasmine groaned as she sat up. "It's probably Spencer again. You know to teach him a lesson I should go over there and open the door as Lady Godiva on her horse."

Everit glanced at her, and one eyebrow shot up, "Lady Godiva?"

Jasmine grabbed her robe and threw it on. "She was an English noblewoman who asked her husband to return some his high taxes to the people, but he said only if she rode a horse naked through the streets."

Everit pulled the blanket over his waist and put his arms behind his head. "Interesting," he smiled up at her.

Jasmine smacked his foot under the blanket, "Don't get any ideas." She pulled the belt tight around her waist and strode over to the door. She pulled it open, and Deputy DuFrain stood there.

He pulled his hat off his head and rubbed the back of his neck. "Sorry to disturb you, ma'am. But I really need to talk to you."

Jasmine stepped back from the door, "Please, come in."

The man stepped inside as he noticed Everit lying in bed with the cover pulled up to his waist. His gaze darted about the room as pink dusted his cheeks.

Jasmine saw he was upset and slightly embarrassed. She placed a hand on his. "Sit down, please. Tell us what's wrong."

DuFrain sat but he squirmed unable to get comfortable, "It's my son, Timmy." He stared into her eyes hoping, praying that she knew how desperate he was. "Something's wrong with him. He doesn't seem to have any energy at all."

Jasmine glanced over at Everit and caught the anger in her man's eyes. She guessed herself that somehow the dark entity was attached to the teenager. She turned back to Deputy DuFrain and sat on a chair next to him. "We'll do everything we can. Our leader Spencer Cross has called for a meeting in about an hour over at Cracker Barrel. We do this to share information," she explained. "I need to know where Timmy's at so we can do what we can for him because I'm going to insist we go over there and maybe rid this town of the trouble that's here tonight."

Everit nodded. This had to end. Children in danger, made him think of little Ouray. He wouldn't let another child die. He thought of Trevor and the other children in the investigations. If they couldn't stop the dark entity, all the children would be in danger.

DuFrain reached into his pocket and pulled out a piece of paper. "I wrote the address down for you already. It's my mother's house. I hope you can do something," the man wiped a hand across his eyes.

Jasmine reached out and grabbed the man's hand in hers. "Both Everit and I will do what we can. Even if Spencer doesn't sanction it."

DuFrain got to his feet, "Thank you both." He excused himself and walked out the door. Jasmine closed the door and locked it. She glanced over at the clock, twenty minutes had passed.

"We're not going to make it if we take individual showers," she announced.

Everit threw the blanket off and strode over to her. He grabbed the belt at her waist and opened the robe. He slid his hands under the robe and ran his hands over her body. A moan escaped her lips when she remembered the meeting.

Jasmine spun around and placed her hands on his chest and smiled to take the sting out of her words as she gazed up at him, "What are you? A rabbit?"

Everit threw his head back and laughed, a rich, hearty laugh. He bent down and brushed a kiss across her lips. "No, my given name is Acalan. It means canoe." His smile and gaze were warm as he watched her and heard her test the name on her tongue. "Do you have another name? A Cherokee name?"

Jasmine glanced away she thought her name was silly. "Adsila, Jasmine Adsila Stone."

"Adsila, it's pretty. What does it mean?"

"Blossom."

Everit ran a hand through her hair, down her back and settled on her hip. "It's a beautiful name, and it suits you."

Jasmine ducked her head and moved away from him. "We'd better hurry. Bella will think I abandoned her."

Jasmine dressed in her usual T-shirt, jeans, and boots. She glanced over at Everit who wore a casual button-down red dress shirt with short sleeves, and tan pants with belt, boots and his pouch hung at his side. His hair hung down to his shoulders. The redshirt made his copper brown skin appear darker.

As they walked outside Bella raced away from Devin and jumped up on Jasmine. Her big paws on Jasmine's stomach. Jasmine played with her a minute. "Were you good for Devin?" Bella woofed. "Good girl." She led the way over to the Escape and beeped the door lock and opened the back door. Bella leaped inside. Jasmine closed the door, and then opened the driver's door and slid into the seat. Everit climbed into the passenger seat.

Jasmine turned the engine over and backed out of her parking slot and followed

Spencer's SUV over to Cracker Barrel. They parked and got out. Jasmine glanced at Everit, "Red looks good on you."

Before they could step away from the Everit Devin bounded to them. "Don't want to leave Bella out," he pulled out a dog-sized vest and hooked it around Bella. He attached the leash and then grinned up at Jasmine. "I got her registered as my service dog, so we can take her into restaurants."

Jasmine goggled at the other man. "When did you do that?"

Devin grinned at her. "When Spencer announced we were coming here. So, I got his keys and drove Bella to City Hall and got her registered as a service animal and she was so good too." He glanced over at the others who were heading to the restaurant. "It appears Spencer is ready to get this meeting started."

Jasmine increased her stride as Everit matched her pace. "I am too. I want to get this over with and get to Timmy."

"Agreed."

Their booted feet echoed across the wood porch style planks as they reached the door passing by rocking chairs that were listed for sale. Everit eyed one and imagined how Jasmine would look cradling an infant. It was painted white but the scrollwork along the back of the chair he liked. He pointed at it. "Before we leave I want to buy that one."

Jasmine glanced up at him, "Really? What do you want with a rocking chair?"

Everit placed his hand on the small of her back, "I like it."

Before she could say anything else, he nudged her through the door. The first thing that met their eyes was the country store section before getting into the restaurant. They walked up to where a woman stood writing down names in a book and how big their parties were.

Spencer stepped up to the woman and simply said, "Cross, party of six."

The woman was going to throw a fuss about the dog with them until she saw the red vest it was wearing that said service dog. She checked and found an out of the way booth away from other customers. She led them through the dining area, past lattice walls covered with old signs, pieces of old equipment used on a farm and framed pictures. She led them to the booth, "Your server will be with you." Bella moved under the table and lay down by Devin's feet.

Roland slid across the bench first, and as Everit began to move down the bench, Roland pulled a cushion out of the bag he brought and slid it down on the bench. Fred saw the movement and rolled his eyes at his friend.

Everit sat down, and a Phhhhhhrt came out from under him. Jasmine sighed, as she sat down. She leaned over to him, "Would you mind standing up for a second?" He did as she asked and sat back down as she grabbed the pinkish cushion.

Jasmine reached around Everit and with a little extra umph she slapped the cushion in Roland's face. The other man broke out laughing as did Fred and Devin. Spencer shot glares at them.

Jasmine leaned over to Everit, "I'm sorry, but you've been pranked."

Everit turned to her, "What is this prank?"

Jasmine glared at Roland and then leaned back. "It's a joke."

Everit understood the concept of a joke. He'd seen warriors before pulling a joke on others. "So, I've been pranked." He turned to Roland, and a grin slid across his face. "Maybe I prank back."

Spencer cleared his throat while they waited for their server. "After going through the journals and double checking with Marcus DuFrain on the events we found the incident. It seems a woman in St. Louis back around 1800 seemed to be disenfranchised with her life. So, she went out and picked some wild arsenic and cooked it with the evening meal. Killing everyone connected to her except for her husband who went to the Sheriff and reported the deaths of his family at the hands of his wife, Lavinia Hull."

Their waitress appeared and gave Spencer the eye and smiled at him. He leaned back and let her get a look at the full package. "What can I get for you?"

They gave her their drink orders, and she turned a walked away from a little extra switch in her hip. Jasmine rolled her eyes.

Fred jabbed Spencer in the ribs, "You old dog."

Spencer buffed his nails on his shirt, the narcissist was back. "Fred, continue with the story."

Fred shrugged his shoulders, "Lavinia Hull fled from St. Louis. She ran down to this area which it was just a very small frontier town at the time. The sheriff followed her, where she'd registered in the small hotel but under another name. The Sheriff probably thought he'd missed her, but he stopped at the town hall and asked for volunteers to help find her."

The waitress returned with their drinks and sat them on the table. "Are you ready to order?" She still had her eyes on Spencer. They placed their orders, and again she swished away.

Roland took up the story, "And it happens that I'm right. Every haunting in this town relates to the death of Lavinia Hull. She's after the children."

Jasmine stared at them. "Good at least we know who she is, but not how she died." Now the difficult part to tell them about Timmy DuFrain and ask them to help her and Everit.

She leaned forward and placed her arms on the table. "At six o'clock we were paid a visit from Deputy DuFrain concerning his son Timmy."

Roland put his hand out on the table stopping her from going any further. "DuFrain was the name of one of the volunteers."

Jasmine smacked a hand on the table, she didn't like being interrupted. "As I was saying, He said there's something wrong with Timmy. He said it was like something was draining his energy and that he's afraid Timmy might die." She pulled the address out of her black bag and set it on the table. "He gave me the address where Timmy is staying at. I want to go over there tonight and check it out."

Spencer shook his head, "Not tonight."

Jasmine's voice lowered as her nostrils flared. Anger oozed through her. "I thought we were here to help people, especially the children."

He nodded, "We are, but we need to know where she died so we can stop her at the source."

Jasmine flattened his lips together. Everit's hand rested on her arm. "Let me take care of this."

He leaned forward, "I can find her for you Spencer. I can find where she's hiding and we can, no we will put a stop to this."

Spencer leaned forward, "How can you find her when they couldn't even catch her in the 1800's."

He saw the waitress coming back with their food. Bella lifted her head from under the table at the smell of the food. The waitress passed them their food, making sure Spencer's was first. She almost slapped the check on the table but then stuffed it into her apron. "I'll just hang onto this just in case you want any," she licked her lips, "desert."

Spencer flashed her his best smile. And he couldn't stop looking at her behind as she walked away.

He cut out a piece of his steak and stabbed it with his fork, "How can you find her." He stuck the fork into his mouth and chewed as he stared at Everit.

Everit smiled as he took a bite of food, chewed and then swallowed. "I'm a psychic medium. If we go where Timmy is I may be able to track her. I believe what's happening to Timmy is like what happened to you. Only Lavinia Hull isn't looking for a person to possess she's looking to kill the children to take her vengeance out on them. I feel," he stared around the room, "I feel that she believes her death was caused by the volunteers."

Jasmine pushed her food to the side. She didn't have much of an appetite now and with Spencer acting like an ass that just compounded the stomach twisting into knots. She focused her attention on Spencer who kept on stuffing his face as if food were going out of style. Moisture collected in her eyes. She wanted to scream, stamp her feet on the floor, and just throw a major tantrum but she was an adult.

She slid out of the seat and walked to the bathroom. She stood in front of a basin and looked at her reflection in the mirror. She turned on the water listening to it splash in the basin and gurgle down the drain. What did she want? She knew what she wanted was to save Timmy DuFrain.

Jasmine cupped her hands under the running water and splashed it on her face. She raised her head up as water dripped from her face. I'm calm, I'll go sit back down and then wring Spencer's damn neck, she thought as she turned the water off. Who was she kidding, she wouldn't do that. She reached out and pulled a paper towel out of a dispenser and dried her face.

Spencer had to admit what Everit said had a ring of truth to it. If he was right and Timmy DuFrain died because of his inaction, then he shouldn't be doing this job at all. "Okay, we'll go."

Jasmine returned to the table a few minutes later. She didn't feel like eating and leaned forward as her brown eyes flashed. If she'd had a shotgun, she would have used it. Instead, she let her words do the equivalent to a shotgun blast. She kept her voice low, "Spencer, your nothing but a sanctimonious ass sitting here trying to get a date so you can get laid while out there is a child who could be taking his last breath."

Everyone stopped eating and looked at Jasmine. A few forks clanked against plates. Even Bella whimpered. Fred looked at the pair, and he grinned. Devin glanced anywhere that was away from the pair. Roland chuckled, and muttered just loud for the others to hear, "Way to go little sister."

Spencer leaned forward, "I'll let that slide this time because you weren't here. I said, and I repeat we'll go."

Jasmine leaned back, some of the knots in her stomach untying but not all. She wanted to leave now. Everit leaned over to her, "You need to eat, keep your energy up."

She shook her head, "I can't. I'm too worried."

As Spencer pushed his plate away from him, their waitress came up to them, "Can I get you anything else?"

"We need a to go box."

"Certainly," she hurried off with visions of Spencer in her head. A couple minutes later she returned with the box. Out of the corner of her eye, she watched Everit put Jasmine's food in it. She placed the check down on the table with another piece of paper under it, and put her hand up to her head like a phone and mouthed, 'Call me.'

They slid out of the booth and Bella joined them. Jasmine looked down at her dog, "Devin, did you feed her anything?"

He grinned at her, "Yep, she had some nice pieces of chicken."

Roland added, "And some steak from me."

Jasmine rolled her eyes and shook her head, "You two are going to make her fat."

Spencer stood in line for the cash register, pulled out his wallet, slid the credit card out of the wallet and handed it to the cashier. He signed the receipt and put the credit card away. "We ready to go?"

Everit spoke to the cashier about holding the rocker he wanted. The woman smiled, "Certainly, sir." He told her his name and gave her his ID so she could write his info on the tag that went with the rocker. She wrote up a new tag and had one of the girls working in the store part hang the sold tag on the rocker.

Spencer glanced at Everit as he strode out of the building with Jasmine hanging on his arm. What did he care, he told himself? But somewhere in his heart, there was a little pang of regret that she wasn't hanging on his arm.

Spencer called out to Jasmine. "I'm dropping Fred and Roland off at the motel so they can get the equipment."

Jasmine replied back, "Sure. We'll meet you there."

Jasmine followed Spencer while Fred and Roland were in the third SUV following them. She gave voice to how she felt, "I'm worried. I have this feeling something will go wrong."

Everit leaned back in his seat, "Relax, we're doing the right thing here, and you know it."

Jasmine glanced over at him as they turned down a street heading to the address. "I know your right, but it's like something's screaming at me to hurry."

She turned off the street into a gravel driveway. The tires crunched across the rock as the three SUV's pulled up to an old two-story farmhouse on the outskirts of town.

Chapter 21

Jasmine looked around as clouds thickened across the sky. Lightning flashed in the distance as a clap of thunder crashed out in a roar. She didn't like it. If this storm hit while they were working it could increase spiritual activity and give the dark entity more power.

Spencer and Devin hopped out of the first SUV, like Jasmine, Everit, and Bella disembarked from the second SUV, and Fred and Roland parked and jumped out of the third.

Spencer turned to Devin. "Make certain you get the DVR, I want this recorded."

"No problem."

Fred, Roland, and Devin hurried with the equipment needed. And joined Spencer, Bella, Jasmine, and Everit at the door. Spencer knocked.

An old woman with gray hair put up in a bun pulled the door open. She wore an old blue flower print dress which hung down past her knees and a pair of slippers. "Yes?" Her face matched the question in her voice as she stared at them.

Jasmine spoke before Spencer could, "Deputy DuFrain sent us to help Timmy."

The woman pulled the door open wider as tears gathered in her eyes. "Please, come in. He's upstairs, poor child." She closed the door and shuffled across the floor to a staircase.

"Last room on your right. It was his father's room."

As they started up the stairs, the woman hollered up. "I'll make us some tea."

Spencer opened his mouth to tell her not to bother when Jasmine put a hand on his arm. "Let her do this. It will keep her mind from Timmy."

They stepped onto the landing of the second story and raced down the hallway to the room where the woman had told them to go. They found a younger woman about the deputy's age hovering over the teen.

Spencer knew Jasmine was better at dealing with people than he was and decided to leave this part to Jasmine as he instructed Fred and Roland where to put the two cameras they brought in with them.

Jasmine approached the woman, "Mrs. DuFrain?"

The woman looked up her eyes filled with tears, fear, and pain as she held her son's hand. Jasmine glanced down, and the teen was so still as if he was in the grip of death already. "What do you want? Who are you?"

Jasmine cleared her throat. "Your husband sent us."

Mrs. DuFrain reached out and gripped Jasmine's hand. "Please, save him."

Jasmine swallowed trying to push the lump that sat hard in her throat. "We'll do everything we can."

Everit stepped over to Jasmine, "You have to examine his aura and see if there's a connection."

Jasmine stepped forward and closed her eyes as she used her mind's eye to examine the boy. She saw it. A tendril of black that encircled the teen's leg. She heard Everit in her mind, "I see it too. This will be difficult. I have to mark him first."

Jasmine opened her eyes and stared up at him, "Mark him?"

Everit nodded, "I have to put holy marks upon his body so I can draw upon the power of the gods to help." He looked over to Mrs. DuFrain. "Would you please remove his clothes down to his underwear?"

The other woman glanced down at her son her expression was pensive as she chewed on her bottom lip. Indecision was her worst trait, and she knew it. The deputy's mother stepped into the bedroom with some teacups and a pot of tea sitting on a tray. She slid it on the desk, "Help yourself."

She took a few steps over to the mother. "Martha, you heard this nice young man. Do as he said."

"But Agnes!"

The old woman crossed her arms over her body. "Either you do it or I will. I may be old, but I can still push you out of the way."

Martha DuFrain, hesitant, her hands shaking pulled at Timmy's undershirt as Agnes pulled the pants off that he slept in.

Everit stepped up to them, "Thank you." He held out a candle and passed it to Agnes. "Would you please light this and put it at the foot of the bed on a table. This will help to light the way."

Agnes took the candle but didn't question him as she moved the bedside table down to the foot of the bed and set the candle on it. Jasmine smiled at the older woman and passed her the lighter she carried, and Agnes lit the candle and passed the lighter back.

Everit turned to Jasmine, "As you start to sever the dark entity from him I will start my part. Together we should be able to free him."

Jasmine took her bag and placed it beside the tray with the teacups and pot. She pulled out the sage bundle, the abalone shell, and an eagle feather. She lit the bundle and then blew out the fire until it smoldered. "I'm ready."

Everit nodded then he began to sing, the song no one had heard for over two thousand years. He pulled out a pot that held white paint he held it up for the world to see and brought it back down. He dipped the fingertips of his index and middle finger into the pot. He started to draw one of the Aztec religious symbols on the boy's forehead.

Jasmine closed her eyes and saw the dark tendril with her mind's eye. She imagined the smoke as an ax that she began to hack away at the vine. But as soon as she got one removed another came to take its place. She remembered what Everit had told her about imagining it to be any type of weapon this time she imagined it was a blazing torch and thrust it into the tendril and burned it away from the aura. She heard a hiss from the room.

Spencer watched what the pair did with fascination. He jumped and nearly shrieked as thunder clapped again but this time it was overhead. Lightning flashed and another clap of thunder. Rain hit the roof and pelted the window.

Everit finished painting a symbol on the boy's stomach and reached the thigh. The same thigh that Jasmine was fighting the more tendrils that made their appearance. As soon as he painted the symbol, the atmosphere in the room changed. It was darker, heavier.

Jasmine took a step back, and Bella growled. The dark entity appeared behind Jasmine. As soon as she turned around the dark mass flowed forward and appeared to rush through her.

Jasmine dropped to one knee, and her hands came up to her chest as she gasped. Her body felt cold. She struggled to push the dark entity out of her. But Lavinia wanted this body. Lightning flashed from outside.

Everit leaned over her, "Jasmine?" Bella continued to bark and growl only at Jasmine. Everit he took a step back, and his song took on a new intensity as he sang. He managed to paint the holy symbol of the snail on her forehead.

Jasmine stood and opened her eyes. They were completely black as she gazed around the room. Spencer stared at her. "Lavinia Hull, get out of her."

She hissed at him and hissed at everyone. Everit turned. "Get the salt, seal her in."

Lavinia focused her eyes on Everit. She smiled at him and licked her lips. "Oh, this will be fun. I didn't know she was one of you." The voice that came out of her mouth wasn't Jasmine's but Lavinia's harsh voice.

She focused Jasmine's eyes on Everit's ensnaring him when Bella jumped and hit Jasmine with her body hard enough to break the contact. Everit sang as Fred and Devin completed the circle of salt around her.

Everit grabbed the abalone shell with the bundle of smoldering sage and picked up the dropped eagle feather. He hurled the smoke at Jasmine. He paused his song to his gods, "Fight her Jasmine you can do it."

Jasmine's body contorted and tears flowing out of her eyes as she held her hands out to the other men from the team. "Can't you see it's me?" Lavinia tried by softening her own voice to Jasmine's.

Everit called out over his shoulder, "Don't fall for her lies. Bella hasn't stopped barking."

Jasmine hurled an insult at him in Cherokee. She glared at Bella.

He continued his song, the lights in the house began to sputter and blink. A light grew on one side of the room followed by another clap of thunder. The lord and lady of the underworld appeared. Their faces were human skulls. The lord wore a huge headdress with long thin feathers that stood up and then flowed backward over his back. His body was emaciated and rail thin. His ribcage could be seen under the black skin. The lady of the underworld her body was supple and firm. She wore the traditional headdress of a queen along with a dress where one shoulder was covered, and the other was uncovered.

In their language, the Lord asked, "What do you require of us, Acalan?"

To everyone else in the room, it looked as if Everit had just dropped to his knees on the hardwood floor. He raised his hands, "Please take the spirit of Lavinia Hull from the body of my wife. Please take her to the underworld so she can never harm anyone else again. She is evil, she murdered her family, and now she wants to take my wife from me."

Mictlanteutli, the lord of the Underworld, clapped his hands together, while Mictlancihuatl joined her voice with Everit's. Lavinia, seeing them resisted. "No, you can't make me leave." A breeze began to stir up around her as Jasmine's hair blew around her face. She tried using Jasmine new-found ability to lock onto the gods in front of her. The only problem, no eyes to focus on.

Mictlanteutli clapped his hands together again, this time so loud it nearly shook the house. "No one refuses," he pulled what would look like the rod but probably more like a staff from his belt at his waist and touched it to Jasmine's head.

The staff glowed, and Jasmine dropped to her knees. "No, keep it away. Don't touch me!" She cried out as the staff drew the spirit of Lavinia Hull from Jasmine, who slumped but Everit caught her before her head hit the floor.

In a flash, the three were gone. Bella stopped barking. Jasmine's eyelids opened, and she looked up at Everit and pressed a hand to his cheek. She didn't have to say the words, he knew. He pressed a hand to her stomach to satisfy himself then pulled her to him and held her tight.

Bella moved over to the pair and licked Everit's hand as if she were giving him her thanks too.

Spencer looked around, "Is it over?"

Everit nodded, "It's over. Lavinia Hull is gone, and she'll never harm anyone again."

Epilogue

Jasmine looked around her, finally glad to get out of this town. She turned around and smiled at Everit as he shoved the last their bags, well mostly his bags in the back of the SUV.

Her attention was caught by a police car and a black town car that pulled into the lot. Mayor Westermann stepped out of the town car, and both the Sheriff and Deputy DuFrain got out of the police car. The deputy stepped over to Jasmine and Everit and stuck his hand out to them as the Sheriff and Mayor talked with Spencer.

DuFrain removed his hat. "I want to thank you both for what you did for my son."

Jasmine grinned at the deputy. "How's Timmy doing?"

"He's driving his momma crazy. He's got his appetite back, and he wants everything under the sun."

Jasmine giggled. She couldn't help but remember what she did to her own mother when she was sick.

The deputy's eyebrow rose as he gazed at her. Jasmine smiled, "Memories of doing the same to my mom."

He grinned at her, "Well, you two come on down whenever you want. We sure are grateful for what you did for our son."

The sheriff strode over DuFrain, Jasmine, and Everit. "I hope you don't mind, but I got your address and phone number from Mr. Cross. Just that when James's trial comes up we're going to need your testimony."

Jasmine took the Sheriff's outstretched hand and shook. "I'll return. I don't want him to hurt another woman ever again."

"Thanks, Miss Stone," he turned on his heel and walked back to his car.

Both cars pulled out of the parking lot of the motel.

Spencer went to the manager's office and settled the bill. He was ready to leave, and everyone climbed into their SUV's. He turned on the communication device that connected all the Escapes to each other.

Jasmine noticed the light blinking and tapped the button on her dash. Spencer's voice came over. "I just wanted to relay that the mayor was very pleased we got rid of Lavinia Hull."

Jasmine grinned at his use of we as Roland's voice came over. She felt sorry for Spencer he'd never live this one down. "You said we, Spencer. So, I guess we're no longer your team."

After several miles of driving, Jasmine glanced over at Everit. "I don't understand why Lavinia Hull went after me. She was going after children."

Everit craned his head and smiled, "Think about it for a minute, and if you haven't got the answer then ask me again."

She thought about it, and then her eyes bulged, and her mouth dropped open when she groaned. "How am I going to explain this to mom and dad?" She placed one hand on her stomach. "How do I explain us to Katie?"

She heard laughter come over the communication system, and then she heard Roland's voice singing, "Jasmine and Everit sitting in a tree…." She slapped the switch off.

About the Author

Wanda Hargrove is a wife and mother of two boys, one of whom is Autistic. She was born and raised in Louisville, Kentucky and still lives there. She's worked different jobs but writing was always a secret passion that she now works hard to achieve her dream of being a successful author. She's worked various jobs.

Kindred Spirits

Made in the USA
Columbia, SC
15 July 2023

20523098R10153